ALONG
THE WAY

A
collection
of sixteen
short stories

HARVEY POOL

outskirts
press

Along the Way
A collection of sixteen short stories
All Rights Reserved.
Copyright © 2020 Harvey Pool
v2.0

This is a work of fiction. Names, characters, businesses, places, events, locales, and incidents are either the products of the author's imagination or used in a fictitious manner. Any resemblance to actual persons, living or dead, or actual events is purely coincidental.

The opinions expressed in this manuscript are solely the opinions of the author and do not represent the opinions or thoughts of the publisher. The author has represented and warranted full ownership and/or legal right to publish all the materials in this book.

This book may not be reproduced, transmitted, or stored in whole or in part by any means, including graphic, electronic, or mechanical without the express written consent of the publisher except in the case of brief quotations embodied in critical articles and reviews.

Outskirts Press, Inc.
http://www.outskirtspress.com

ISBN: 978-1-9772-2698-3

Cover Photo © 2020 www.gettyimages.com.. All rights reserved - used with permission.

Outskirts Press and the "OP" logo are trademarks belonging to Outskirts Press, Inc.

PRINTED IN THE UNITED STATES OF AMERICA

To Susan

Contents

Introduction

I began writing these stories over thirty years ago. Sixteen stories in almost a third of a century isn't a prodigious output. My explanation (excuse) is that I wrote whenever available time and inspiration converged. Most of my time and effort in the past was applied to my jobs as creative director/owner of advertising agencies, as a partner in radio stations and in raising my three children. Later, my wife and I owned and ran a fine art gallery. After I mostly retired ten years ago, I was able to devote more time to creating short fiction.

The earliest of these stories is "Connecticut Wedding." "The Serious Game" followed two years later. All the other stories presented here were written over the past five years.

My focus is narrow. I write about what I know from my life experience. But it would be a mistake to conclude that these stories are strictly autobiographical. Certainly, they reflect feelings, ideas and sometimes events of my long life. Apart from that observation, I advise the reader that this is fiction, not memoir. My objective is to write imaginatively about intimate experience that offers universal insights. I hope that I've achieved that goal at least some of the time.

Biography

Harvey Pool was born and raised on the North Side of Chicago. He attended elementary and high school in that city and graduated from the University of Illinois at Urbana-Champaign.

For many years, he owned and operated advertising agencies, radio stations and fine art galleries.

Mr. Pool has lived in Chicago and Los Angeles. He currently resides in Chicago with his wife, Susan.

Uncle Leo

My uncle Leo is a sad man—a good man but unhappy and cranky too. My experience is that almost all of the eighty-year-olds I've known are cynical about what my dad used to call "the human condition." But Leo's behavior went well beyond run-of-the-mill existential despair. I'm not a psychiatrist, but I would have to say that Leo was deeply depressed.

He lived alone on the top floor of a three-flat apartment building on Bell Avenue in the Chicago neighborhood of Rogers Park. Leo, my aunt Millie and their two children, my cousins Larry and Nora, had moved into the three-bed-room, one-bathroom apartment in 1958. Aunt Millie died six years ago in 2008. Larry is a lawyer in Los Angeles. Nora was killed in an automobile accident when she was eighteen.

Leo complained bitterly about how his neighborhood had gone to hell. How all the "towel heads" made it seem like he was living in Calcutta or Lahore, although he had never been to these places. Still, Leo continued to live in the Rogers Park apartment—continued to plow up the three flights of dimly lighted stairs even though the climb had become increasingly difficult for an old man suffering from arthritis and diabetes.

"One of these days, Max, I'm going to drop dead on these stairs. Or maybe the stink of the Paki cooking will kill me," he told me.

Leo hadn't always been this way. I remember that he rarely missed any of my baseball games when I pitched for Senn High School. It was Leo who taught me to throw a curveball. Leo who took me to at least a half dozen Cubs games every season.

My dad, Sam, Leo's only sibling, wasn't much of a sports fan and didn't have any free time. He worked seven days a week running his downtown currency exchange. Leo, however, liked to say that he was his own boss. As an independent representative for three furniture manufacturers, Leo proudly told me that he worked on his own time schedule.

He was a lifelong Cubs fan, and I suppose that it was inevitable that he passed along that disease to me. If you don't follow professional baseball, I need to explain that Cubs fans are a special breed—reflexively loyal followers of a team that hasn't won a World Series in over a hundred years.

The truth is that I was Leo's only friend. Most of his old gang had died or moved somewhere warm so that they could avoid Chicago's punishing winters. Those few who remained weren't especially eager to spend time with Leo. Not surprising because, to be fair, Leo wasn't exactly a walk in the park. Except for his undiminished regard for the Cubs and Israel, he didn't much care about anything.

Somehow, though, Leo and I got along. In fact, after my dad died, Leo and I became even closer. Probably because I was his only real family. As for his son, Leo had a long-ago dispute with Larry, and they hadn't seen each other for over ten years. Although Larry had tried to reconcile a couple of times, Leo was stubborn and petulant.

"Look, he's got his life in LA, and I've got mine. The last time I saw him, he acted like he was doing me a big favor. He kept looking at his watch. So, let it be. I don't need anything from him."

I made a point of having lunch or dinner with Leo once a week. For lunch, I'd pick him up at his apartment to make sure that his place wasn't a total mess and that he had enough food on hand. Then, I'd drive us to the Bagel Deli on North Broadway. Leo's order never changed: half a lean corn beef on rye and a bowl of matzo ball soup. Once in a while, I persuaded him to get a whole sandwich and to take the un-eaten half back home. For dinner, I'd take him to my home in Highland Park where he'd spend a few awkward hours with my wife, Janet, and my two boys, Tommy and Sean. I say "awkward" because my kids were not especially interested in Israeli politics—Leo's main subject of conversation other than the Cubs, and unfortunately, my sons were into soccer, not baseball, and in spite of my urging, neither had a dot of interest in the Cubs.

"Soccer! Only foreigners play soccer. What's wrong with baseball?" Leo asked.

Tommy and Sean were polite, but clearly they were convinced that Uncle Leo was pretty weird. Janet just rolled her eyes.

It was early April when I got a phone call from Donny Gordon at my accounting office. Donny is an old friend and an internist. He's also Leo's and my primary physician.

"Hey, Donny, I already had my annual checkup and passed with flying colors. Are you trying to rustle up some more business or did you just misread my test results?"

"You, I'm happy to say, are in excellent health. I'm calling about Leo. I'm not sure I'm doing the right thing telling you, but I'm concerned about him, and I think that you should know about it."

"What's wrong?"

"Look, he suffers from bad arthritis like a lot of elderly people. He also has diabetes, which is pretty much under control. It's not the physical stuff that worries me. It's what's going on in his head."

"What do you mean?"

"I think he's suicidal."

"I know he's kind of bitter, but suicide?"

"Well, he never said it in so many words, but he says things like, why is he just hanging around—just taking up space?"

"I think maybe he's just talking. You know, just lonely, not suicidal."

"Max, he asked me what would happen if he took a whole bunch of his Hydrocodone pills or injected too much insulin."

"Jesus!"

"Max, you've known me a long time. I'm no alarmist. I think you need to be concerned. "

"Did you talk to him about maybe seeing a shrink?"

"I mentioned it, and he told me very firmly to forget about it. Then he changed the subject."

"What do you think I should do?"

"He likes you, Max. As far as I can tell, you're in a group of one, so he might listen to you. Frankly, there's no one else."

———————

Leo woke up as usual about three thirty for his first piss of the night. He'd been dreaming again of Millie—of how they used to go to Cubs games. How she loved Mr. Cubs, Ernie Banks. How they'd sit in the bleachers and how she'd get sunburned even wearing her big floppy hat and applying tons of suntan lotion. He loved those days . . . could almost feel the warm sun on his face. Now he shivered in the early April night and cursed his cheap Paki landlord for shutting down the heat this early in the year.

This was the worst time of the night for him because once he was awake, it was hard for him to get back to sleep. So, he lay there—cold and stiff with arthritis. And he worried. Not so much about dying—not the actual end of life. He was pretty much ready to call it a ballgame. What worried him was the prospect of a long, painful death, of wasting away in some nursing home—warehouses for the old and dying, he called them. His mother had spent the last two years of her life in one of those dismal and costly dumps. The last year, she didn't even know who he was. He didn't want to wind up that way.

Face it, he didn't have much going for him. He made a mental checklist: Health, lousy. Friends, except for Max, zero. Money, running out. Why was he hanging on? He had had his day, and now the best thing to do was to leave the scene while he still had all of his marbles—was his own man—not some zombie. Five o'clock—time to piss again.

———

Donny Gordon's phone call had a strong impression on me. But I didn't have any idea of what to do to deter Leo from his suicidal scheme, if that was what he really had in mind. Confronting him directly wouldn't work. Leo would just shine me on. He was too wily for a direct approach.

A solution to the Leo dilemma popped up from an unlikely source: the long-losing Chicago Cubs started the season by winning their first ten games. That's right, ten wins, no losses. The media was beating the drums. The pennant-starved fans were already talking World Series. I was even more than a little excited myself. Most important, the Cubs' strong start had brought some sunshine into Leo's life. Even the April weather was cooperating with seventy-degree temperatures and no rain.

I scored two tickets for the first game of the Cardinals series. Not cheap. Cubs tickets, usually fairly easy to get and not expensive this early in the season, were now a hot commodity. Although Leo tried to act blasé about the Cubs' great start, I could see that he was excited to go to the game, and when the Cubs won two to one in the ninth inning, I actually heard my world-weary uncle croak out the Cubs victory song:

"Go, Cubs, go! Go, Cubs, go! Hey, Chicago, whadda ya say, the Cubs are gonna win today."

When he caught my amused reaction, Leo gave me an embarrassed smile and said, 'What the hell, Max. They're eleven and zip."

By the All-Star break in July, the amazing Cubs were sixty-five and fifteen. I'm not kidding! They were leading the division by ten games and had the best record in all of baseball. Leo and I had already been to six Cub games. Most of all I had never seen Leo so up. He even looked a lot better, his usual gray pallor replaced by a kind of ruddiness. And Donny Gordon informed me that Leo's last checkup was the best he had had in years. And not a word from Leo about the futility of his life. All he could talk about was his Cubs.

"I'm not saying they'll go all the way, but they got a hell of a team. They're playing like a real solid ball club. Let's put it this way, I'm hopeful."

———◉———

If this were a fairy tale, the Cubs would win the pennant and the World Series and Leo would become the happiest, friendliest guy in the city—kind of like Scrooge in *A Christmas Carol*. But this story is about the Cubs and Chicago.

In early August, the Cubs dropped nine games in a row. They went from doing everything right to doing about everything wrong. Pitchers couldn't throw a strike. And when they finally did, the batters crushed the fat pitches they got. Cub batters went from being sluggers to just being slugs. Infielders couldn't catch a ball, and when they did, their throws were rarely in the vicinity of their intended destinations. Outfielders lost fly balls in the sun on cloudy days. The manager, whom the media had praised as a genius, was now proclaimed to be an idiot. The players, all of whom had been the best of pals, now suspected each other of various kinds of personal treachery and plotted revenge. The general reaction among Cub fans was along the lines of that it had all been too good to last—after all, they pointed out, it was the Cubs. And so it went through the entire month.

Remarkably, Leo would have nothing to do with all the bad-mouthing. When I expressed my disillusionment, Leo scolded me.

"Come on, Max, don't quit on them now. Remember, when the going gets tough, the tough get going."

"The tough get going? Where did you get that?"

"Don't be a smart-ass. The Cubs have been my team all my life. I'm telling you that they can get the magic back. We all gotta hang in there."

Frankly, I was so impressed that a big-time depressive like Leo wasn't spiraling back down into a black funk that I determined not to desert Leo or the Cubs. If Leo could remain optimistic, who was I to lose faith.

And surprise, surprise, the Cubs started to play better. No, they weren't playing the way they had in the first half of the season, but they got better. At least they were winning more games than they were losing. By Labor Day they were neck and neck with the Cardinals for the division lead. Then they took two of three from the Cardinals and swept Cincinnati in another three-game series. With about a month of the season to go, the Cubs were on top of the National League Central Division, and Leo was a man on a mission.

"I feel it, Max. I really do. They can go all the way. I know they always fold, but I honest to God believe that this team is different."

And you know what, maybe they were, because they wrapped up their division title the last week of the regular season when they took a two-game series from Houston. The Chicago Cubs were in the playoffs.

Our winners opened the playoffs against the Los Angeles Dodgers, a powerhouse that had won 101 games during the regular season. The oddsmakers had the Cubs as an eight-to-five underdog. Leo and I watched the opener, which was played in Los Angeles, from my home in Highland Park. The Cubs looked nervous, and it showed. They lost six to zip.

"It's just one game, Max." Leo admonished me. And when they lost the second game, two to one on a wild pitch, Leo was undeterred.

"I'm not bailing out, and you better not either, sonny. The game coulda gone either way."

"Coulda gone either way? Come on, Leo, what a cliché."

"So what! I'll give you another one. You gotta believe."

What concerned me most was that, in spite of Leo's bravado, one more loss would eliminate the Cubs and might have Leo figuring out how many Hydrocodone pills it would take to eliminate himself.

I managed to get two tickets to the Cubs opener at Wrigley Field from a friend who knew someone who knew someone. The price was about the same as one of my monthly home mortgage payments. Leo was so excited I worried that he would have a stroke before we ever got to the ballpark. We arrived an hour and a half early. The scene around the Wrigley Field was electric. For those of you who don't know, Wrigley Field, unlike almost all other major league ballparks, is located in a vibrant neighborhood on Chicago's North Side brimming with a wide variety of restaurants, bars, stores, apartment buildings and condos. Wrigleyville, as it had come to be known, had become kind of upscale. When I was a kid, it was pretty much blue-collar. I'd been to games at some of the new mega ballparks. To me, they felt like those huge shopping malls isolated from the real life of the cities around them. Wrigley was, and still is, something else altogether. Relatively small and old. Capacity just north of forty-two thousand. The outfield walls are covered in ivy, and the field is real grass, the kind that's planted and grown, not manufactured.

When we climbed the stairs from the artificially lighted area of concession stands under the stadium and emerged into the bright October light, Leo stood still and surveyed the field and the stands already filled with ecstatic fans and shook his head in wonder.

"It's amazing. I've been coming to this place for maybe seventy years, but I still get the shivers every time. It never changes."

I squeezed my uncle's shoulder.

"Let's see some baseball, Leo."

The game turned out to be a slug fest. The Cubs hit four homeruns and the Dodgers two. Final score, Cubs ten . . . Dodgers six. The Cubs were still alive, and so very much was Leo; although, by the end of the game, he was so hoarse from screaming, he could barely talk.

"Maxie, we're still in it. Hell of a game," he rasped.

The next game was a pitchers' duel that the Cubs won two to nothing, tying the series at two all. The deciding game would be in Los Angeles. Leo and I had lunch on the travel day at the Bagel. Leo couldn't stop talking to me and to everybody else in the deli, including our middle-aged waitress, Brenda. He actually flirted with her.

"What's with him?" she asked me while Leo was gabbing with another customer.

"For years he's Silent Sam, and now he's all of a sudden Mr. Personality."

Leo told me that he wanted to watch the deciding game at his apartment.

"I love your kids and Janet, but I don't want any distractions. Anyway, when we watched at your house last time, they lost. I'm superstitious."

"Your place is okay by me."

I didn't want any distractions either. Especially if Leo went berserk or dropped dead during the game. Also, Leo had a new, big-screen television—the only new thing in his apartment.

The game was one that would be talked about for years. Our Cubs, down five to two in the eighth inning, tied it in the ninth and then scored the go-ahead run in the eleventh. The Dodgers had the last at bat, and when they loaded the bases with only one out, I think I heard my atheist uncle mumble a prayer. The next Dodger batter hit a sharp ground ball back to the pitcher that the Cubs nimbly turned into a game-ending double play. Leo was not a hugger, but after that final out, he crushed me in an embrace that actually took my breath away.

"What did I tell you, boychik. You gotta believe."

The Chicago Cubs were division champs and would now move on to the National League Championship Series.

———=((◦))=———

There was a two-day hiatus before the start of the seven-game National League Championship Series. I was glad, because I needed a rest after all the craziness of the Dodgers-Cubs battle. Not Leo. He was like a politician running for office—glad-handing everyone—calling people he hadn't seen in years, replaying the highlights of the last Cub victory. He even complimented his Pakistani landlord on his landscaping ability. Definitely Mr. Personality.

The Cubs opponent in the league championship was the Philadelphia Phillies. They were a hot ball club, having swept their division series with Atlanta. As a matter of fact, the Phillies had won eighteen of the last twenty games they had played. Worse yet, they had pummeled our boys during the regular season by taking seven of eight games. Vegas made the Cubs a nine-to-five underdog.

The Cubs and Phillies split the first two games, which were played in Philadelphia. Leo was very positive about that result.

"All we gotta do now is win our home games, and we're going to the World Series. No problem."

But the valiant Cubbies lost the opener in Chicago. It was a well-played game on both sides with the Phillies edging us three to two. Leo cautioned me to remain calm—that this was only a temporary setback.

I had finagled tickets to the second home game. Let's not talk money. What I will tell you is that Leo pressed five one-hundred-dollar bills on me and said, "I know this has been costing you an arm and a leg, Max. I want you to know I appreciate it. I'm not a schnorrer. This won't pay you back for everything, but maybe it'll help."

The game, what can I say, it was pure joy—a blowout, with the Cubs winning eleven to two. The Cubs never looked better—Leo too. And the good vibes carried over to the next game, which the now confident North Siders took five to three.

Heading back to Philly, our boys were up three games to two and needed only one victory to put them in their first World Series since 1945.

Possibly just about everyone in Chicago was beyond nervous, desperately hoping that this would be the magic year that the Cubs would finally win it all but dreading the wrenching disappointment of a Cub collapse. Could you blame them? Remember this was a ball club with a long,

long history of failure. But not this time. They marched into Philadelphia and scored five runs in the first inning and proceeded to beat the hell out of the Phillies. Final score, Cubs twelve . . . Phillies two. The confident Cubs were World Series bound. Their opponent, winner of twenty-seven World Series and the most renowned team in baseball history: the New York Yankees.

I expected Leo to go nuts—like everyone else in the city, the state of Illinois and a good part of the United States—but he was as calm and composed as a general preparing for a great battle. He meticulously reviewed with me each of the Yankees, including pitchers and utility players—noting their strengths and weaknesses and comparing them quite objectively to their Cubs' counterparts. His conclusion: the Yanks were better on paper, but the Cubs had the edge in intangibles.

"We got destiny on our side, Maxie."

And Leo told me something else that shocked and pleased me. He said that he had phoned his estranged son, Larry, and that he was glad that they had finally talked.

"It's funny, Max. I don't even remember exactly why we stopped talking. I know . . . sometimes I can be a jerk, but what am I waiting for? I'm eighty. He's the only kid I have left. It's time."

The next day I got a phone call from Larry. He asked me if I could get three tickets for one of the series games and offered to pay for all the tickets. And he told me not to tell his father that he was going to fly to Chicago for the game. I told him that I appreciated his generous offer but that I didn't expect him to pay for everything.

"Please, Max, don't misunderstand. I don't want you to think I'm acting like a big shot about the tickets. I know they're very expensive. I'd just like to do something for Dad and for you too."

"I'll tell you what, Larry. If I can even get tickets, you pay for your ticket, and we'll split the price of Leo's."

"That's very considerate. Let me know the date as soon as you can. Just leave my ticket at will call, and I'll meet you both at the seats. But don't let Dad know I'll be there."

"I won't say a word."

I pulled every string I could, begged and pleaded and finally was allowed to hand over a small fortune to buy three not-so-very-good tickets far down and high up along the left-field line. We had our three World Series tickets to game number four at Wrigley Field.

I gave Larry the news, and he told me that he would arrive in Chicago late the night before the game and would, as planned, meet Leo and me at our seats. Again, he told me not to tell Leo about his coming to the game.

The Cubs played well in the first two games at Yankee Stadium, but the Yanks played better. The New Yorkers won both games—the first four to two and the second a heartbreaking loss when the Yankees scored two runs in the bottom of the ninth inning to edge us three to two.

Leo and I, as usual, watched both games at his apartment. He remained calm, even strangely subdued, even when the Yankees rallied to win game two. At the end of the game, he spoke to me as a seasoned commander might to one of his officers after losing a skirmish.

"Don't panic, boy. We lost a battle—not the war. This is

a seven-game series. We've only played two, and we got the next three back here."

"Lose the battle—win the war. What is that? Another saying from the Book of Leo Berns?"

Leo allowed me a half smile.

When the Yanks crushed us in the opener at Wrigley Field to take a three-to-nothing lead in the series, the mood in the city reflected the dark storm clouds that were forming over Lake Michigan, and I was relieved that I had tickets to game four because I feared that there might not be a game five.

Leo, though, was spouting an anthology of bromides, which included: Back to the Wall, Darkest Before the Dawn, Take It One Game at a Time and the aforementioned You Gotta Believe.

"We're their lucky charm, Max. Remember, we haven't lost in the playoffs when you and I are there. And tomorrow, we're gonna be there, and we're gonna win. Count on it."

It rained that night—a cold, steady rain—and I worried that the game would be called off. But by morning, the sun rose on a clear, crisp autumn day.

Although the game wouldn't start until two, Leo told me to pick him up at noon. When I pulled up to his apartment building, he was already waiting downstairs.

Ordinarily, he wore an old, beaten-up Cubs cap, but to-day he sported a Cubs jacket as well.

"I didn't know you owned a Cubs jacket, Leo."

"I've had it for years, but I only wear it for special occasions like today. Millie gave it to me."

"Well, you're looking good, Uncle."

We got to our seats about an hour before the start of the game, and the ballpark was already packed and thick with a loud blend of excitement and hope. Even the rooftop stands that lined Wrigley Field along Waveland and Sheffield Avenues across from the ballpark were crowded with noisy fans. I couldn't help but wonder what they had paid for their long-distance viewing privileges.

It was only ten minutes before game time, and I was getting anxious. Larry wasn't here. Maybe his flight got delayed. Maybe the rain. Maybe there was some kind of screwup at will call. Maybe I should phone him. Then, as the announcer instructed the crowd to stand for the singing of the national anthem, a tall, bald guy holding an obviously brand-new Cubs cap quietly slipped into the space next to Leo and touched his arm.

"Hi, Dad."

If you're lucky, sometime in your life—maybe for a minute, maybe for an hour, maybe for an entire day—everything comes together, and you're absolutely happy. You feel that the gods have smiled especially on you—that you've got it all figured out. No problems. No worries. No fears. Perfect peace and exhilaration all at once. This afternoon was one of those extraordinary times.

The Cubs played flawlessly and humbled the mighty Yankees six to one. The cheering never stopped. High-fives all around. The stranger sitting next to you was your best pal. You loved the Cubs. You loved everyone in the ballpark and outside too. And maybe the happiest of the happy was Leo. He laughed. He screamed. He talked nonstop to his son, Larry. By the end of the game, father and son were finishing each other's sentences, kidding, joking, recounting old family stories. Leo was telling everyone in our vicinity:

"Hey, I got my son here—came in all the way from LA to join me. Go, Cubs, go! I'm gonna spend some time with him out there this winter. Maybe you can introduce me to a movie star, Larry."

The following night, the three of us gathered at Leo's to watch game five. I wish that I could tell you that the Cubbies made history by staging the greatest comeback in

World Series history. They didn't. They lost that night. The Yanks were champs again. But it didn't matter, Leo told us.

"Wait till next year."

To Die in Chicago

S o, Asher was going to die in Chicago. Ironic, he thought, after all the years—all the women, the divorces, the fame and money, the gossip, the booze and drugs. All the movies he had made, the places he had worked all over the world: Los Angeles, New York, Aspen, London, Rome, Paris, Beirut, Tel Aviv and other points on the map that had dimmed in memory. After all that living, to end up back where he began eighty years ago in the city of his birth and youth. God, if there was one, must have a bizarre sense of humor.

The diagnosis was not exactly a surprise—his heart had been failing for some time. His energy fading. Yet the finality of the doctor's verdict was a shock. The incongruity of his morbidity and the clear salutary summer sky over Lake Michigan visible from the twenty-second floor of his room at Northwestern Memorial Hospital struck Asher as another bad joke—on him. For some reason he couldn't fathom, he wondered if the Cubs were playing today not far away at Wrigley Field.

"Do you have family, friends you might want to contact, Mr. Asher?" Dr. Kim asked.

"No family. I had a sister, but she's gone now. One old Chicago friend who, sorry to say, I haven't seen in a long time. A couple of ex-wives who will miss the alimony I pay them. Me, not so much."

"No children?"

"I had a son, but he was killed in Iraq."

"I'm sorry."

"Me too. So, Doc, what now?"

"I'm afraid that you're a poor candidate for a heart transplant. There is medication that will help some, but the honest answer, Mr. Asher, is that I recommend that you make arrangements for either a nursing home or perhaps hospice care."

"Sounds grim. How long do I have?"

"It's hard to say."

"Give it a try."

"Two, maybe three months."

Asher had traveled to Chicago from his home in Los Angeles specifically to see Dr. Kim, who specialized in treating late-stage heart failure. Other than stops at the airport, he had not been back to Chicago since his mother died twenty years ago. Only a handful of mourners had attended her funeral. How many would be at his? His agent, a scattering of actors and others in the industry with whom he had worked through the years, his accountant, probably some reporters. Close friends—he had had a couple, but both had died last year. So, not much of a representation in the old-pal category.

"Look, Dr. Kim, there is a person who I'd like to see here in Chicago—some places I want to visit. Do you think that I'm up to that?"

"You'll need someone to drive you, but if you don't over-extend yourself, you should be all right—for a while."

After Dr. Kim left, Asher was calm—no panic or fear. What the hell, his health had been lousy. He was eighty. He didn't expect miracles. Nor did he believe in an afterlife—a heaven or hell. He had lived his life. There had been good and bad parts. He couldn't say that he had no regrets. He did—plenty. But he figured that he would have probably made the same mistakes given another chance.

Asher had no intention of ending his days in some de-pressing, foul-smelling nursing home surrounded by incon-tinent droolers and indifferent attendants. His mother and father had died in those sad, expensive human dumps. Not for him. He didn't need two, three months for what he want-ed to do. He checked himself out of the hospital and into a suite at the Peninsula Hotel just off Michigan Avenue.

The concierge arranged for a driver to pick him up at the hotel the following morning at ten. Asher would have pre-ferred to start earlier, but he knew that it took him about two hours to get himself together after he woke from a night's sleep interrupted by at least three trips to the bathroom. The bathroom dominated his night and especially his first waking hours. A bowel movement alone was usually a forty-minute project. The consumption of fourteen pills followed by a shave and shower left him with perhaps thirty minutes to carefully dress himself. Getting into shoes and socks was a painful challenge. One cup of coffee and a toasted English muffin and he was more of less ready when the driver rang at ten.

The driver's name was Pablo Gasca. He wore a fashionable

dark-blue suit and white shirt and a maroon tie. His black loafers were polished to military standards. Asher guessed that he was in his late twenties. He spoke without an accent.

"Good morning, Mr. Asher. I understand that you'll need me for most of the day, but I don't have a specific itinerary."

"Let's just kind of freelance for today, Pablo. Is it okay to call you Pablo?"

"Pablo is fine, sir."

"Good. You know, Pablo, I grew up here in Chicago around Devon and Western in Rogers Park a long time ago. I haven't been back here in quite some time, and though I know it sounds strange, I'd like to visit, make that, revisit, some of my old haunts."

"I don't think that's so strange, Mr. Asher," Pablo said with a pleasant smile. His teeth were very white and regular except for one eyetooth, which was slightly crooked.

"Okay, then, let's start with the apartment building where I lived from the time I was five until I went away to college." Asher gave Pablo his old address on Oakly Avenue.

"I know exactly where that is, Mr. Asher. My brother lives just a couple blocks away on Claremont."

"How about that. Our building was a three-flat. We had three bedrooms and one bathroom, which we shared with my mom and dad, my sister and my grandparents."

"That pretty much describes my brother's place except no grandparents living with them. Instead he has four kids."

"What's that old line about the more things change, the more they stay the same—or something like that."

The old Oakly building hadn't changed that much nor had the other apartment buildings on the street. But it seemed to him that everything looked a bit run-down—lawns needed tending, and he saw graffiti on several garages and porches off the alley behind the buildings.

"You know, Pablo, we used to play softball in these narrow alleys. The only thing is you had to hit the ball up the middle. If you pulled the ball, it was sure to land on a garage roof. A valuable player was someone who could quickly climb a garage and retrieve the ball."

Pablo smiled. "I don't know if they're still doing that."

"Probably not. Kids have Little League now and coaches and all kinds of equipment. Organized. It's a different world. I forgot how close together the buildings were. Now I see that these passageways between buildings can't be more than maybe ten feet wide. Our bathroom window looked right into our neighbor's bathroom. The Panizies. They kept that window open halfway, and that's how I saw my first naked woman—girl, really. Virginia Penizi was, I think, fifteen—a real woman to me at eleven. She was drying herself after a shower. I could hardly breathe. In almost seventy years since, I don't think I've been so aroused. I hope I haven't embarrassed you, Pablo."

"Not at all. I like your story. When did you leave Chicago, Mr. Asher?"

"After college at the University of Michigan. I got a job in Los Angeles. I wanted to be in the movie business."

"Is that what you do?"

"Did is more like it. The movie business is for young people. I haven't made a movie in ten years."

"I'm a big movie fan. Would I know any of your films?"

Asher named three.

"Oh my God, you're Jake Asher. The company didn't give me your first name. I love those movies. You're kind of a legend."

"It's been a long time since I had a hit. I'm surprised a young man like you remembers me."

"I go to DePaul Law School at night, but I'm a movie fan. I've taken a couple of acting courses at Steppenwolf, and I've been in a few local commercials."

"Stick with law school."

"You seemed to have done pretty well, Mr. Asher."

"I'm not complaining, but it's a tough business, Pablo. Lots of competition and hard on family life. Do you have a girlfriend?"

"Kind of. We've gone together since high school. She teaches third grade. She wants to get married, but I don't think I'm ready for that responsibility."

"It's a big move. I had a girlfriend in Chicago. Met her at the University of Michigan. She lived with her family on Lake Shore Drive. Molly Weiss then. It didn't work out. My fault. She married a doctor—Molly Becker now. I haven't seen her—even talked to her—in about sixty years. But I'd like to see her, if she'll meet me. I kind of kept track of her, so I know she's still around. Nothing romantic. I'd just like to tie up some loose ends."

"Sixty years is a long time, Mr. Asher. You could be disappointed."

"Her too. I'm certainly not the man she knew. Hard to believe now, but I was a good-looking guy back then. I've been thinking about her—about how it didn't work out. I know I'm being foolish, but I'm running out of time."

"I think I understand how you feel. I suppose you're never going to get—what is it called, closure—until you call her. Just don't expect too much."

"You're wise beyond your years, young man. I'll call her."

But what would he say? "Hi, Molly, it's your old boyfriend, Jake, who promised his eternal love and then ran off to La La Land, never to return. You remember Jake Asher from whom you haven't heard a word in six decades. So, how you doing?"

She would certainly hang up. Who could blame her? Molly had sent him a letter back then seeking answers, clarity. He could offer her neither, so he had remained silent—for six decades. Mute. Gutless. Now what did he want from her? Forgiveness? Understanding? Yes, Molly might understand and forgive. But what he desperately longed for was much more, and Asher knew it was unobtainable. He wanted to go back in time. To recapture precious emotions, the evanescent feelings of first love. The madness, the electricity, the passion, the heartsickness, the heartbreak, the hope. Asher wanted it all back, and he knew it was impossible. He thought, hoped, that Molly might be at his mother's funeral. And when she was not, he was far more disappointed than he had expected. He remembered verbatim words they had spoken a lifetime ago. Conversations about their secrets, their dreams, their fears, the most honest and intimate of his long life—maybe of Molly's too. Perhaps he simply wanted to hear her voice again—to see how she looked before he died. He phoned.

"Really, Jake Asher, my unbelievable God! Where are you?"

"In Chicago—in a car, actually."

"It's been a lifetime, Jake Asher. I used to imagine this conversation and all the things I would say, but now I don't know what to say. Why are you calling me?"

"I know, Molly, this must be a shock. As you said, it's been a long time—and that's my fault. I've thought about calling you a thousand times but couldn't find the courage."

"So now you've found the courage?"

"I left things between us in a bad place. I know that. I'm not getting any younger. I was hoping to straighten out some old stuff."

"Just like that after sixty years?"

"You make it sound stupid."

"Do you blame me?

"No. Look, Molly, once we were close. I've thought a lot about you for a very long time. I don't expect us to all of a sudden become best buddies. I'm eighty years old, and I'd like to at least try to make things between us a little better."

"You think a phone call can do that?"

"Let's just say, I was hoping to make a start."

"And now that's important to you?"

"Yes, that's why I called you."

"Jake, I'm a little old for new starts. I have a life—a good life, which you are not part of. It took me a long time to get over the hurt when you left my life. And I don't think that I'm up to having you in my life now."

"Molly, I'm not looking to become part of your life. I just want you to know that I'm sorry that I let you down way back when. I was young and selfish. It makes me happy to know that you have a good life—it truly does—and the last thing I'd want is to cause you any trouble."

"I'm human, Jake, and I'll admit that I'm curious to find out what your life has been like—to just possibly mend old hurts. After all these years, I'd probably kick myself if I told you to get lost. How long are you in town?"

"I'm not sure."

"Maybe you would like to have dinner with my husband, Al, and me? We live in Glencoe. From what I've heard, you're single—again. If you have a friend, please bring her."

"No friend, but I'd very much like to see you and your husband."

They made a date. As Pablo guided the car along Lake Shore Drive, Asher watched for a moment the busy green tennis courts at Waveland—the joggers, bikers and roller-bladers on the park path, the sailboats that seemed to float in the distance on the lake he had known since childhood.

A new start at this stage of the game—foolish, but somehow he felt an all-but-forgotten sense of exhilaration.

Connecticut Wedding

J anice kissed his neck softly. "I love you, baby."
"I love you more," Paul answered.

"No you don't," she teased.

"Okay, it's a tie."

They had arrived in New York the night before. Now they were dressing for the wedding that they would attend that afternoon.

"I bet Joanne is beside herself," he said.

"I bet you're right, but she's had enough time to make up her mind. They've been living together for, what is it . . . four years?"

"It's been a long time since I've been to Connecticut. The drive, as I recall, is beautiful," Paul said.

"They're getting married in a two-hundred-year-old church. It should be lovely."

"Do you have Joanne's directions? I think I know the way, but the directions won't hurt."

"I have them right here," Janice answered. "You know Joanne, she wrote a small book and also included two maps."

"Great, you be the navigator, and I'll drive."

They left the hotel, gift in hand, well-scrubbed, well-dressed, full of a sense of well-being. A handsome couple, they held hands waiting for the garage man to bring their rental car. It had rained during the night, and the morning air smelled fresh and clean, although the sky was muddy and threatening.

"The doorman told us that to get to the Triborough Bridge, we have to go to Sixty-First and get on the East River Drive. That shouldn't be too tough," he said.

They had no trouble getting to East River Drive. Chattering about the good fortune of being together on this small adventure, they passed through the toll gate, followed the Route 95 signs north to New England and missed the Hutchison River Parkway exit that they had clearly been instructed to take.

About ten miles later, he suspected that a mistake had been made.

"Honey, weren't we supposed to turn at Hutchison Parkway?"

"We haven't come to it yet," she answered.

"Are you sure? I think Joanne said it was only a couple of miles."

"Maybe we did miss it, but it's okay because Joanne says that we can stay on 95 until we hit White Plains."

"That's one of the things I like about Joanne," he said, mildly scolding. "She figures that you'll get screwed up and gives us an option."

"No harm done. Want to hear some music?"

Janice searched the dial from left to right, rejecting rock, country, jazz and classical programming before settling on a format of middle-of-the-road music.

"As usual, my darling, you pick elevator music."

"I'll ignore that . . . Look for Route 287. That's our next turnoff."

"Roger," he answered. "You know, Jan, this is beautiful country, so green. It's amazing how rural it is around here, and we're just 45 minutes from the city."

"Honey, better turn right here at Westchester Parkway and head for the Tappen Zee Bridge."

He swerved the car quickly into the right-hand lane in order not to miss the turnoff.

"Jesus, Janice, do me a favor and tell me more than a few seconds before I'm supposed to turn."

She rolled her eyes dramatically.

"Don't panic . . . We've got plenty of time. You don't need to drive like crazy."

"I'm not driving like crazy, but I didn't want to miss the exit, or we'd wind up going twenty miles out of our way."

"That's better than getting us killed."

"Okay . . . let's make a deal: you tell me what to do, say, five minutes ahead of time, and I'll drive very carefully . . . okay?"

"Okay, okay."

They drove silently for a while, successfully crossing Route 287 to Merritt Parkway North into the rolling, verdant Connecticut countryside.

"Do you think they'll be happy?" she asked.

"I don't know. Joanne seemed kind of lukewarm to me. Nick's been after her for a long time. I find him to be a good guy, but Joanne has a sort of sour attitude. I don't know why he's so eager to tie himself down with her."

"Why do you say tie down?" Janice asked. "You know marriage doesn't have to be that way. I think that they have real feelings for each other."

"I don't know . . . Maybe you're right. I just don't know of too many marriages that are great successes."

"There are some. Anyway, watch for exit forty-nine north."

"How far is it?" he asked.

"I'm not sure. Have we come to Fairfield?"

"You know, you do this all the time, Janice. You're supposed to keep on top of things. I don't remember if we've passed Fairfield or not."

"I beg your pardon, my lord. I thought that you'd be able to drive and look at road signs simultaneously."

"Look, you don't have to do a lot . . . Just sit there and check the map and watch the signs," he snapped.

"Don't make such a big deal about it."

"I'm not making a big deal. I just hate getting lost."

"Okay, there's the Fairfield sign. Thank God we're not marooned here in the wilds of Connecticut."

"Very funny."

For a time, they drove without talking. The radio filled the car with an old Barbra Streisand ballad.

"I love weddings," she volunteered.

"Every time we go to a wedding or even hear about one you start."

"Start what?"

"Oh, come on! Start hinting . . . maybe *suggesting* is a better word, that it might not be a bad idea for us."

"I never hinted . . . suggested that. I told you when we

started living together that there was no pressure on either of us to do anything. Anyway, I'm not about to push you or anyone into marriage."

"That's reassuring," he answered.

"You know, sometimes you can be a real shit."

"Look, I don't want to fight. It's a pretty drive, and it should be a nice day. I just get annoyed when I don't know exactly where I'm going. I'm sorry."

"You can only do what you can do, Paul."

"What does that mean?"

"It means that you can only feel what you're capable of feeling."

"Meaning, I suppose, that I'm not capable of feeling much."

"Paul, every time you really get close to a genuine feeling, you run the other way and hide."

"And if I don't want to get married, that means that I have no real feelings?"

"You just can't make a commitment to anyone. I don't think that it's just me. It's anyone who comes close to you."

"Thank you, Dr. Freud."

"That's so typical of you," she said. "Sarcasm. That's a lot easier than honesty."

"Time out! How do you turn on the wipers? In case you didn't notice, it's raining."

"Remember, I'm the navigator. You're the pilot. Figure it out."

"God damnit! I can't see a thing," he shouted.

"Oh, pull over and figure it out. It's not a calamity."

"It could be if I can't see where I'm going."

After a few minutes of fiddling with the instrument panel, they inadvertently turned off the radio, activated the hazard warning and finally managed to locate the wiper control. It was raining hard when he pulled the car back onto the highway.

He spoke first.

"Look, let's not get into a battle. Just don't try to analyze me. We get along fine except when you push me."

"Push you! I simply want to have a serious conversation."

"I don't want to upset you. I just don't feel like getting into a long, involved discussion about the merits of marriage. Unless I agree with you, you get pissed. So, let's talk about something else," he said.

"I see . . . end of discussion because the subject doesn't please you. What should we talk about . . . the lovely scenery . . . the nasty weather?"

"For starters . . . how about how do we get where we're going? I have no idea now where we are."

"Just keep on Merritt Parkway. We have a ways to go."

They continued without conversation, the awkward silence broken by the clap of the wipers and the sigh of the wheels on the wet pavement.

"What am I looking for?" he finally asked.

"Exit forty-nine."

"How far is it?"

"I think about ten miles."

"Let's make up before we get there. I don't want to put a damper on the wedding."

"Neither do I. It's just that you get to me sometimes, Paul."

"Meaning that I'm the cause of the argument."

"Meaning that we seem to want different things . . . that we're heading in different directions. I don't know, I need more than you can or want to give."

"What more? We get along. We usually like each other. You know we're not kids. Both of us have been through this before. As I recall, those marriages were pretty lousy. Consider the possibility that marriage, as an institution, isn't such a good thing. What the hell is wrong with living together the way we do?"

"It doesn't lead anywhere. Paul, I'm thirty-five years old. Maybe I want children, a family. I don't want to be alone."

"We're together. You're not alone," he answered.

"We could be together until you got tired of the arrangement . . . find someone else, and then you'd move on. You see that kind of thing all the time."

"How does marriage make it different? My God, most of the people we know are divorced."

"Don't you want more? A family? Something more permanent?" she implored.

"I tried it once. It was a total failure. But you know something funny? I remember having a conversation just like this with her before we got married."

"Sometimes I really hate you."

"Thanks . . . Let's just cool it, okay? We can talk later. I don't want to upset Nick and Joanne."

"You're so considerate, Paul."

They turned at exit forty-nine north to Danbury. Their only conversation was her terse directions and his perfunctory acknowledgment. The rain had stopped, but the electric crackle of thunder rumbled on the horizon.

They arrived at the old church early and joined several other guests who were being greeted by the groom.

"Nick, my boy. There's still time to escape," Paul said, perhaps a bit too loudly as he pumped the groom's hand.

"Too late, pal. Glad to see the two of you. Did you have any trouble getting here?" Nick asked.

"Not a bit," Paul answered.

"Hey, what's this, Janice . . . tears I see on that beautiful face of yours?" Nick asked.

"Oh, you know me, Nick. I always cry at weddings."

The Serious Game

They had not intended to go to the park, but after they started for the office, Les had said that it was such a nice day, why not handle their paperwork at the park. And after all, it was Saturday, and they planned to work only a half day.

Myron had agreed. It was a beautiful morning, one of the perfect Southern California variety that is the secret envy of the rest of the country, especially in the winter when most parts of the United States are suffering blizzards or freezing rain or some other meteorological misery. This January morning, the temperature nudged into the high seventies. It had rained the night before, and the cloudless, blue sky was washed of any trace of smog. A bright sun peaked over the snow-capped mountains to the east and bathed the immaculately tended lawns in warm amber.

Roxbury Park occupied a square block of Beverly Hills real estate. A baseball field, two basketball courts, tennis courts, running path, playground, two lawn bowling greens, the grass manicured even more precisely than the park's putting greens, all ringed by the tidy beds of tangerine-and-white snapdragons and magnolia trees.

Although it was not yet ten, the strollers, dog walkers, sunbathers, joggers, readers, teeter-totterers, putters, bowlers, lovers and families were already in place.

Les and Myron sat at a picnic table and signed documents. First one would sign then pass the paper to the other for his signature. There were several documents concerned with pension plans and tax returns. The two men were partners in a certified public accounting firm. They had been friends since both were high school students more than thirty years ago. They had grown up in the same Chicago neighborhood. Played on the same teams. Dated many of the same girls . . . had many of the same friends, then and now. Both had moved to Los Angeles after college.

"You know, I can always tell a Chicago softball player," Les said, watching the Little League game. He didn't expect a response from Myron.

"He's the guy who doesn't try to pull the ball. He lines the ball up the middle. You know why? Because we played in the alleys. You couldn't pull the ball, or it would wind up on a garage roof. You had to hit the ball right up the middle."

"Jimmy Baranco was the best I ever saw at that," Myron said.

"Yeah. Do you ever wonder what he's doing now?"

"His father was a plumber, and I think he took over the business."

"Do you remember his sister, Emily? What a pair of tits," Les said.

"She married Sherman Kaplan. Remember what a

big stink that was. The Kaplans were Orthodox, and Mrs. Baranco was just about a nun."

"My brother lives on the same block with them now in Highland Park. Sherman's an attorney. God, they've been married . . . it's gotta be twenty-five years," Les said.

"In those days, Sherman was the best basketball player on the North Side."

"That's because there weren't any blacks there," Les said.

"True, but he was a hell of a ball player."

"Can you imagine a six-foot-three-inch center today?"

"Yeah, but Sherman could stuff."

"Remember in warm-ups how the band would do a drum roll and Sherman would soar up there and slam dunk," Les said.

"Now they've got five-foot-eight-inch guards who can do it."

"I know, but it was a hell of a thing then," Les said.

<hr/>

They watched a young couple walk by. Her fingers hooked the back pocket of his jeans. His hand casually held the back of her neck.

"So, how's it going with Sheila?" Myron asked.

"Same stuff. She's unhappy. Both of the kids are out of the house away at school, and she's unhappy . . . unfulfilled . . . depressed."

"Is she still talking about divorce?"

"We've been seeing a marriage counselor. I don't know,

maybe she's helping us to communicate. That's the key word today—communicate. Anyway, I'm trying. I guess Sheila is too."

"And it's working?"

"Who knows. You're lucky, pal; Enid and you never had any trouble."

"You know Enid," Myron said. "She never gets upset. Nothing ruffles her. Sometimes I'd like to see something get to her."

"Be glad she's like that. I'd give you one week with Sheila, and you'd go bananas."

For a while, the two friends watched the Little League game. The smack of leather, the crack of the ball meeting bat, the chatter that hadn't changed in a hundred years drifted across the park. Overhead, a small plane hummed on its way to Santa Monica Airport.

"It's amazing, Les," Myron said after a while. "These kids, what can they be . . . ten, eleven years old. They've got coaches and uniforms. Everything is so organized. Look at that diamond. It looks like the Dodgers' ground crew takes care of it. We didn't even play hardball."

"Yeah, we played with that big sixteen-inch softball . . . the clincher. It was hard as a rock in the early innings . . . Then it got kind of mushy."

"Sid Handler died."

"My God, when, Myron?"

"Yesterday. My mother called me. He was jogging and had a heart attack. That was it. I should have told you right away but . . ." Myron's voice trailed off.

"Sid's our age . . . maybe a few years older. I saw him in

Chicago last June when my sister was in the hospital. He looked okay."

"My mother said that he was under a lot of pressure . . . that he had lost a lot of money in commodities. He was in that business, you know."

"Jesus, that's terrible. It makes you think. It's scary. I think of myself as being about twenty. Oh, I know in my head that I'm not, but it just doesn't really register. Do you know what I mean, Myron?"

"Yeah, I do." Myron said. "But sometimes the truth pops up. You know Alice with the terrific ass. She's Bernie's new administrative assistant . . . No one's a secretary anymore."

"The one who always wears the tight jeans?"

"Right. Well, I was talking to her the other day, and we got around to ages. She's something like twenty-four. So I asked her to guess my age. I figured she'd say about forty-five. She looks at me carefully and says, 'Oh, Mr. Becker, I'd say fifty-five.' I just nodded and didn't say anything."

"At least she didn't say sixty."

"Let's take a walk," Les said. "My back hurts when I sit too long."

They strolled past the tennis courts. The *pock, pock, pock* of the ball against strings punctuated by exclamations of "Great shot!" or "Just out!" The green fence screening prevented the accountants from seeing the players. In a few minutes, they came to the basketball courts. There was a kinship among all playground basketball players. The relationship held whether they played in Beverly Hills or in Harlem. Women had not yet broken into the playground game. This was a man's game. Perhaps a boy's game. They came to the playground . . . young men to seriously hone and test their skills . . . others, now out of school or work, to reassert their self-worth, their manhood . . . and some well into their middle years, their hair thinning and lives thickening, to capture a touch of a much simpler, perhaps happier time.

This morning, two serious games were in progress. Both were half-court contests involving three players on each side. The rules had not changed much in fifty years. The winners held the court, taking on all challengers until they were defeated or until they decided to give up the court. There were no uniforms or referees. Outfits included shorts of a hundred varieties, from cutoff jeans to official National Basketball Association issue. Shirts were optional. If the weather was warm, they were often eschewed. When worn, T-shirts dominated, most emblazoned with the names of such establishments as Sepi's Giant Submarines, Four Deuces Bar, various schools and assorted musical groups.

"Jesus, look at that!" Myron said as he watched a young black man leap to pluck a lob pass almost even with the basket's rim and in the same motion gently drop the ball through the basket.

"The kid's good," Les replied. "Let's watch for a while."

"Do you think about your health?" Myron asked. "I do . . . a lot. I never used to, but now I do. The funny thing is, you know me, I'm never sick."

"Myron, we all think about it more now. I used to worry

about my hair, but that doesn't bother me anymore. Anyway, I heard that bald men are supposed to be sexy."

"Well, as you get older, you take care of yourself a little more. It's natural. We used to play ball all day. Now we sit on our asses. I jog ... you play racquetball. We stop smoking. We try to stay in shape."

Les nodded approval.

On one court, a mild argument was going on. A very tall, skinny teenager was insisting that he had been fouled.

"I had all-ball, man," a somewhat older, bearded man replied. "But it's your call."

Les watched and thought about Sid Handler. He hadn't seen much of him in recent years. Sid lived in Chicago and Les in California. It was hard to believe that Sid was dead. It made him sad and frightened. He had known Sid all his life, and now Sid had no more life. Les had gone to his bar mitzvah. Should he go to his funeral?

No ... better to send a condolence card to his wife. He hardly knew her. Laury was her name, he thought. Funny, her name. Once, long ago in high school, he and Sid had gone to the lake one humid summer night with two girls they had met at Riverview Amusement Park. Hot stuff. They felt sure they would score with these two. But they had not. The name of the girl Sid had figured was hot stuff that Chicago August night was Laury. Later, Sid had married another Laury. Riverview Park has been torn down. He couldn't remember the name of the girl he hadn't scored with that night. Now Sid was dead.

"You want to shoot a few baskets?" Les asked Myron.

"I haven't played in about ten years."

"It'll come back to you."

"Lester, my boy, you were a shooter. I never could shoot worth a damn."

"True, but it'll give us some exercise."

Two men, they appeared to be in their twenties, were casually shooting baskets on one of the courts that wasn't being used for either of the serious games. One was black of medium height, the other a short blond who appeared to be a gymnast or weightlifter. His powerful upper body looked like it had been placed on the trunk and legs of another, much smaller, man.

"Do you guys mind if we shoot some baskets with you?" Les asked.

The black man, Sam, studied the two middle-aged accountants for a few seconds, then turned to his muscular companion.

"Doesn't make any difference to me. You care, Andy?"

"Nah, but we got winners as soon as they finish on the other court."

Sam bounced the ball to Myron, who dribbled it cautiously to the free-throw line and let fly a line-drive shot that careened off the backboard.

Les retrieved the ball and tried a short jump shot that circled the rim and dropped out. His legs felt heavy. The two young men checked the progress of the serious game. Andy yawned.

Myron wondered what he was doing. Basketball had never been his game. He couldn't handle the ball very well, and his shooting had always been terrible. He felt awkward now...a balding, middle-aged man. *These two kids must think*

I'm ridiculous in my walking shorts and sandals. When the ball came to him, he passed it to Les or to one of the young men. He was surprised when Les asked their two playmates if they wanted to play a game.

"You mean the two of you against Sam and me?" Andy said.

"Yeah, just a short game while you're waiting for the other game," Les said.

"He doesn't have shoes," Andy replied, pointing to Myron's sandals.

"It's all right. He'll be okay," Les said.

"Sure," Sam said. "It's fine with us. You guys want to take it out?"

"That's okay. You can take it out first," Les said.

As Andy and Sam proceeded to start the game, Myron spoke confidentially to Les. "This may not be the greatest idea you ever had."

"It's no big deal. We'll get a little exercise . . . have some laughs."

"The laughs I'm sure of," Myron said.

"Myron, you take the short guy. I'll watch the black guy, Sam."

Andy took the ball out-of-bounds and passed it nonchalantly to Sam, who returned it to Andy. Myron positioned himself defensively directly in front of Andy about fifteen feet from the basket. Andy made a feint to his left, then quickly dribbled right. Myron reacted to the feint and was left behind as Andy dribbled to the basket for an easy layup.

The move was repeated, except this time, Andy faked right and dribbled left, resulting in another layup.

Myron defended somewhat better the third time and stuck closer to Andy, preventing him from making a layup. Andy's missed shot, however, was rebounded by Sam, who scored an easy follow-up basket.

"What's the score?" Andy yelled over to the court where the serious game was in progress.

"Six all," someone shouted back.

In the next few minutes, Sam made a jump shot and Andy a stylish reverse layup. Myron and Les had yet to touch the ball.

"Jesus, my legs feel like rubber," Myron whispered to Les. "How you doin'?"

"I'm sweating like a pig. We're really playing shitty. These guys aren't that good."

"We're not exactly the Lakers."

In truth, Myron and Les were now playing better defense against the two young men. Sam tried a jump shot that Les, a couple of inches taller than the black man, was able to barely tip. The errant shot fell short of the mark but was grabbed by Andy, who leaped high and hooked the ball over Myron's outstretched arms. The ball bounded off the back rim back into Andy's grasp. His second rebound shot was successful.

"Shit!" Myron shouted in disgust.

"Seven nothing's a shutout, man," Sam warned.

"You guys mind if we get a quick drink?" Les asked.

"No problem," Sam answered.

When they reached the nearby drinking fountain, Les put an arm around Myron's shoulder. "Damn it, Myron, I don't want to be a shutout. These guys aren't that good. I just don't want to get blitzed."

"I'm not exactly trying to let the little muscleman score."

"I know, I know. I'm workin' hard too. I just don't think they're that much better than us."

"Okay, big guy," Myron said.

Before the game resumed, Sam checked the score of the serious game, which was reported as nine to eight.

Andy got the ball and started to dribble with his back toward the basket. Myron held his round, and Andy was forced to a position farther away from the basket than he sought. When he terminated his dribble, Les quickly came over to double-team Andy. The short man attempted to pass the ball to Sam, but Les was able to block the pass and capture the ball. For the first time, the two old-timers had the ball on offense.

Les took the ball out and threw it in to Myron, who set a pick for Les at about the free-throw line. With Myron between him and Les, Sam was unable to prevent Les from taking an unguarded jump shot. The ball hit the front rim of the basket and was rebounded by Myron, who passed the ball back to Les, who had moved closer to the basket. Les made the follow-up. The accountants would not, at any rate, be shut out.

Their first score seemed to give Les and Myron a lift, and in the next few minutes, they scored three baskets . . . a jump shot and tip in by Les and a two-handed set shot by Myron. The latter missile, a relic of a bygone era, had never been seen by the two younger men.

"Nice shot, man," Andy said.

"What score you got?" Sam shouted to the other court.

"Twelve all," came the reply.

In the early going, Sam and Andy had been casual in playing the two older men. They were, after all, waiting for the serious game, and the two old guys, one bald and wearing sandals and the other with graying hair and a pot belly, had not seemed to require much effort on their part. But the old guys were playing hard, and it aroused the young men. They stiffened their defense and forced Myron to fumble the ball out-of-bounds.

"All right, you guys," Sam said. "We got you now."

Confidently, Sam threw the ball to Andy. But Myron, using an old playground ploy, whirled around and intercepted the pass and fed the ball to Les, who scored unguarded.

"Son of a bitch!" Andy yelled. "Pay attention, Sammy!"

"You old guys are sneaky," Sam said.

"Yeah, you gotta watch us every second." Les gasped.

"Let's just play," Andy said impatiently.

The younger men's defense was now tenacious, and it forced the accountants to work hard to get an open shot. Finally, Les took a long jump shot that bounced tantalizingly on the front rim of the basket and fell off. Andy leaped high and secured the rebound. Les struggled to catch his breath. Myron's feet burned.

Andy dribbled to the free-throw line and turned to the basket. He waved Sam away and made it clear that he wanted to isolate Myron . . . to make Myron guard him one-on-one. The unspoken declaration was clear. *I can score on this man. He cannot, on his own, prevent me from scoring a basket.* Andy broke quickly to his right, then deftly dribbled behind his back, changing the ball to his left hand. The move gave him a half-step lead on Myron. But the bald man moved fast and made up the disadvantage. Andy, nevertheless, lowered his overdeveloped right shoulder and banged into Myron as he got off an off-balance shot that missed its target.

"Foul," Andy yelled.

"I thought I had position," Myron protested.

"Bullshit . . . you were all over me."

"Hey, relax, it's your call," Myron said.

"You charged. You ran right into him," Les said.

"No way."

"Cool it, Andy. You jumped right into the man," Sam said.

"You guys got winners," someone shouted from the other court.

"Yeah, be right there," Sam answered. "Sorry, guys, we gotta go. Nice game."

"Yeah . . . you guys played good. I'm sorry I got pissed. Good game."

"No problem. Thanks for the game," Myron said.

"Yeah, thanks." Les said.

"We didn't do too badly," Les said as the accountants headed for the car.

"We held our own," Myron said.

"How do you feel?" Les said.

"Not bad. My feet hurt, but I feel pretty good. How about you?"

"My back is starting to stiffen up, but otherwise, okay. We were comin' on. I think we could have beaten 'em." Les said.

"Maybe so."

Les squinted in the bright, warm sunlight.

"You want to do this again ... maybe next Saturday?"

"I have to get the right shoes," Myron said.

"No question ... With the right shoes, we'll be ready to play in the serious game."

What the Dog Knew

A dog sees and hears a lot that humans don't. I'm not talking about distant sounds or the occasional shy rabbit or a furtive rat; I mean what's really going on inside a home—private stuff like arguments, lies and heartbreak. A dog is pretty much invisible on those occasions.

I'm a four-year-old male Weimaraner, and I've been witness to more than you could ever imagine. My name is Jason, and I live with my human family in a handsome four-bedroom townhouse in Chicago's Lincoln Park. My family, the Platts, consist of Jim and Sarah Platt and their three children—Amy, age eight; Wilson, eleven; and Marci, sixteen. Lately there's been trouble in the Platt household. Jim and Sarah's marriage is on the rocks.

I was a puppy when the Platts got me. Back then, things were peaceful, but recently life has become rocky. Jim and Sarah fight all the time, and some of the battles are scary to me let alone to the three Platt children. Some of the fights are about Jim not coming home until late at night. Sarah hates that. Jim tells Sarah to stop nagging him.

"Get off my back. You don't have a problem spending the

money I make. I don't work for the post office. I'm a lawyer. Sometimes I have to work late."

"You said you'd be home no later than seven, and you get here at ten thirty. And you don't even call or answer my calls. Do you even care about me or the kids?"

"Yeah, I care, and if you did, you'd stop screaming at me. It scares the kids. For Christ's sake, you've even got the poor dog shaking."

And I was. You have to remember that my life is completely dependent on my owners for just about everything: food, of course, but especially for attention and affection. And when things are going bad in the family, everyone suffers.

Sarah suspects that Jim is seeing another woman. She's not sure, but I am. Jim takes me for walks late at night and calls the "other woman" on his cell phone. Her name is Margo. She's a lawyer too. It's obvious that they're crazy about each other, but their conversation is embarrassing to listen to.

"I hate this, Jim. All this sneaking around. Where are we going with this?"

"I know. It's not easy for me either."

"This is not what we said it would be—a good time for both of us. Fun, good sex, no complications. Now it's gotten out of control."

"I didn't plan for us, you know, to get so involved."

"Well, we are, and it's not fun. You're married, Jim. I'm not. You've got a wife and kids. I don't want to do this."

"I don't have great answers. It's terrific when we're together and awful when I can't see you. And I know I'm hurting all of you. You think I like this?"

"We can't go on like this. I won't."

"Look, let's step back for a while. The Labor Day holiday is next week. You said you were going to spend time with your folks. It'll give us a chance to think things through. We need some quiet time."

This conversation wasn't unique. As a matter of fact, it was very much like plenty of others that I had heard over the past few months. I sniffed the early autumn breeze from Lake Michigan and pretended to be on the lookout for squirrels. Jim scratched behind my ears and spoke softly to me.

"You got the good life, Jay boy. No worries. No problems. Well, let's head back to the war."

Humans are like that. They never realize that when they have problems, we dogs are affected too.

———— ᐳ•◉•ᐸ ————

Everyone will tell you that stress can make you sick, and that goes for dogs too. After Labor Day, nothing changed. Jim and Margo couldn't bring themselves to break up. They fought. The Platts fought. The kids didn't know what was going on, but they knew that there was trouble at home. And I got sick to my stomach. I threw up everything I tried to eat. And sometimes it happened right there in the posh townhouse. A definite no-no for a usually well-behaved four-year-old family pet.

"What is wrong with you, Jason? Sarah scolded as she reluctantly inspected my smelly mess there on the cherry wood floor. You haven't puked since you were a puppy."

If I could talk, I'd tell her that the pressure of living with all the strain of the Platt family drama was getting to me. Dogs have nervous stomachs just like humans.

It was after my third "accident" that Sarah brought up the subject to Jim at breakfast one crisp and cloudy Saturday morning.

"We have to do something about Jason."

"What do you mean?"

"He's been barfing all over the place."

"He has?"

"Yes, for the last couple of months."

"That's not like him. Maybe we should take him to the vet. Why didn't you say something?"

"You're such a busy man, I haven't had a chance to talk to you."

"Hey, I'm not looking for an argument. I'll take him."

"Are you sure that you have the time? I mean, with your heavy schedule."

"Don't be such a bitch. I said I'd take him."

And Jim did. Dr. Marks had been my vet since I was a puppy, and I liked him. He treated me like an old friend.

"Well, Jason. Let's see what's going on with you."

Then the good doctor gave me a thorough examination: gently probed my tummy, checked my eyes, ears and mouth, took my temperature, even got a blood sample. When he finished, he patted me and spoke to Jim.

"Maybe the blood sample will show something, but I doubt it. There's nothing physically wrong with this dog. Something else is bothering him. This is one tense dog, and that's not like him. Is there something going on at home, Jim? Dogs have a way of knowing."

"I don't know—maybe. Sarah and I have some issues, but it's not like we take it out on the dog."

"You'd be surprised how much dogs pick up—kids too."

The situation in the Platt household cooled down a bit as the Chicago autumn moved toward winter. Jim and Sarah observed a fragile cease-fire and made plans for the traditional family Thanksgiving celebration, an event that would include both Platts' parents and Jim's brother and his family as well as Sarah's sister and her family. All together, seventeen at the Turkey Day table.

My late-night walks with Jim continued, and so did his conversations with Margo. But somehow the dialogue was different. There was a change in tone. I could feel it.

"So, Mar, what are you doing for Thanksgiving?"

"Not much. I'll spend the day with my brother and his family in Wheaton."

"Sounds good."

"Not really, but I don't have anywhere better to be. And you?"

"We have this big family thing we do every year. You know how that goes."

"I'm not sure that I do, but you have a good time. I've gotta go."

"Don't be like that. I'll miss you."

"Yeah." And then Margo ended the call.

"That's great," Jim said to no one but me.

We continued our night amble through the frigid streets of Lincoln Park. It had snowed during the day, and now slippery patches of ice made footing tricky. We made our way along Fullerton, turned south at Clark and stopped at the corner of Webster. Jim pulled me close to him.

"What the hell am I supposed to do?"

I could see his breath in the night air.

"What am I gonna do?"

Neither of us was paying attention to the car that barreled through the red light, fish-tailed on the invisible ice and struck us with the skidding rear-end of the car. The driver regained control, stopped for perhaps ten seconds and then sped off into the darkness. My first thought was that that was a close call. The maniac had barely touched us. I was half-right. Jim was unhurt, but when I tried to run to him, I collapsed. My right front leg lay folded under me at a grotesque angle. I was about to vomit again.

After the accident, everyone was especially nice to me, and I must say that I took advantage of all the sympathy. Oh, I certainly had some pain, and the cast on my leg itched and prevented me from getting around very well, but I sort of overdid the suffering. I think that Jim felt guilty even though he hadn't been responsible for the car hitting me. To be honest, I enjoyed all the attention. Sometimes a dog is taken for granted by his human family. Now I was the main recipient of kindness and consideration. I'm not saying that the Platts were ever anything but good to me, but now the whole family was focused on my recovery.

"To tell you the truth, Sarah, I just wasn't paying attention. I shoulda seen the car coming. It's lucky both of us didn't get killed. I don't know—my mind seems to wander lately."

"I've noticed. So have the kids. Wilson asked me the other day why you've missed a bunch of his basketball games. He said that you used to be there all the time. I told him you were very busy at work. He kind of shrugged and said that other dads must work hard too, but that they still are there at the games."

"I'll make it up to him. I'm gonna talk to him."

"I think that would be a good idea." Sarah hesitated. "I'm sorry to say it, Jim, but for a long time, even when you're here, you're not. You seem to be somewhere else or want to be somewhere else. I see it, and I think that the kids do too. Don't you want to be here, Jim?"

"Why would you say that?"

"Jimmy, we've been married for eighteen years. I think I know you pretty well. You've been different lately. I'm not a fool. I know when you're unhappy or unsatisfied or whatever it is. Is there someone else? I'd rather know than go on with all your discontent."

Tears ran down Sarah's face and dripped onto the oriental rug right next to where I was lying on my doggie blanket.

"There's no one else. I'm just tired—very tired. I know that I haven't been much good to you and the kids for a while. I see that now. I just need some time. There's a lot going on, and I need to slow things down—to refigure some things. Can you do that for me?"

"I can try, but I, we, need to resolve this one way or the other. I'm scared and sad and angry, and I don't want to be like this."

"I understand. Just give me a little time."

It seemed so clear to me. Why couldn't he see it? *You're a smart guy, Jim. Figure it out. You've got a good wife and kids. They love you. That's a lot to be happy about. You want to throw it away for what—the possibility of a new life, a sexier life? What are the odds that it will work out? We dogs are accused of acting on our base emotions. Well, it appears to me, Jim, that you've been thinking with your dick, not your head.* In certain ways, guys are a lot like dogs.

———————

I love the Christmas season. The neighborhood all aglow with multicolored lights, the Christmas trees filled with wonderful ornaments proudly on display in big picture windows. The ribboned and wrapped gifts under the trees. That pine fragrance in the falling snow. Even the sappy Christmas carols. Call me a sentimental hound, but the whole Christmas scene makes me feel happy and optimistic.

My leg was much better too—no more cast, and although I was still a little gimpy, I didn't have much pain. And the mood around the Platt household was improved, more upbeat. Jim and Sarah weren't exactly hugging and kissing, but they weren't at each other's throats either.

"I appreciate your talking to Wilson, Jim. Since you did, he's a different kid. He's stopped moping around and has actually started talking again."

"I should have had that conversation with him a long time ago. I'm sorry that I've been such a shitty father lately . . . and I know I haven't been a great husband either."

"You used to be. Are we going to be okay, Jim?"

"We'll be fine."

I would have to say that that conversation gave me reason to feel that things were looking better, but who can be sure what humans will say or do when it comes to sex. Jim was smitten. Frankly, I wasn't certain what would happen.

Jim and Margo had agreed, after two postponements, to meet, as Margo put it, "to once and for all to make a decision." I wish that I could tell you that Jim came across as strong on the phone, but he didn't.

"You know how I feel about you, baby. I just want to do right by everybody. I hope you understand. This is not easy."

"Change is never easy, Jim. I understand that, but I'm tired of waiting around. Either you're in or you're out. You need to make a decision."

"I've got to take the dog to the vet Saturday morning. I'll be done by ten. We can meet at the park on North Avenue just off Clark. There's a fountain at the corner of North and Clark almost next to the history museum. I'll be there by say 10:30 at the latest. It'll give us some time to work things out. Is that okay with you?"

"I know the place. I'll be there, but, Jimmy, I want you to know—I never wanted it to come to this, all this melodrama, like a stupid soap opera. Either we've got a future together or we don't. I'm sorry and kind of afraid that it comes down to this, but I guess it has. I'll see you Saturday morning by the fountain."

As you might imagine, I was a nervous wreck Saturday morning. Dr. Marks examined me and pronounced me physically fit but noted that I seemed to be a bundle of nerves and that so did Jim. But he discreetly probed no further into the cause of our anxiety.

On the drive to the meeting with Margo, Jim talked to me or maybe to himself nonstop.

"No way I can do this. I mean, I know what's right. Right? I got to do the right thing. What is the right thing? Okay, I know. Why the hell couldn't we just have a regular affair, you know, all the good stuff—nobody gets hurt. Instead I get super involved. Something is wrong with me. Well, I'm at the end of the line. Stop it! Be a man! Tell her so long—it was terrific, but it's just not to be. Margo will understand. No, she won't. But she's a survivor. She'll be okay—even relieved in a way. Jesus, Jimmy, you're pathetic."

By now we were almost there. Jim headed down Dearborn. It was snowing hard, big flakes blowing against the windshield, the wipers clicking in fast rhythm, the drone of the heater blending with the classic music from the radio. It was hot in the car. I panted and felt sick to my stomach. Jim clicked off the radio and turned west onto North Avenue. His hand trembled as he stroked my neck. Margo was the only one at the fountain. Her white parka stood out against the charcoal sky. Jim slowed the car almost to a stop. Margo started toward the car. Their eyes met for an instant. Then Jim slowly shook his head side to side and drove home.

Posterity

The old man wrote almost every morning. He fixed his breakfast of hot tea, yogurt and one slice of rye toast and consumed it along with the nine pills that were required to treat his various maladies: heart, kidney, arthritis.

By the time he settled at his desk, a rose-tinted sun was rising over Lake Michigan. His wife, Janice, would not wake for another hour. He closed the door of the den so that he wouldn't disturb her. He wrote in longhand, although, he was computer literate, unlike some of his contemporaries. The tactile sensation of his pen scratching words on paper pleased him. Since he had retired seven years ago as a partner at a midsized Chicago law firm specializing in real estate transactions, he had written a novella and twenty-three short stories. He wrote about life as he had known it—about real characters he had encountered along the way, about the hopes and disappointments of these men and women. He strove to illuminate their personal stories—their dreams, their failures and their sometime triumphs. His aim was to capture this panorama with skill and honesty. He wasn't sure that he had succeeded.

He had just finished another short story, "To Die in Chicago," his best, he thought. Two of his stories had won honorable mentions in respected short story competitions, but none of his work had been published. He was considering self-publishing a collection of his stories but had resisted doing so, hoping a publisher, preferably a prestigious one, would market his work. So far—no takers. Nevertheless, the old man, his name was Michael Bliss, though disappointed, was not discouraged. He knew that the odds of his becoming a successful writer at age seventy-five were not good, but he had hopes.

When he first started writing, it had been an interesting hobby—a creative outlet. But his writing had grown in importance. Now, in a way, his stories had become his legacy bequeathed originally to family and friends, and later, as he thought the strength of his prose had developed, he aspired to a larger audience and to posterity. He read widely and well and understood and appreciated literature. Appraising the quality of his own work, however, was difficult, but he felt that his best efforts had merit, and he believed that he was improving. When he reread his novella, written seven years ago, he could see substantial progress in his work. It seemed to him that a good deal of contemporary fiction published in magazines and short-story collections was no better than his best unpublished work. But he kept that conceit to himself.

—————⇒«(◉)»⇐—————

His most important source of encouragement came from

his old friend Nathaniel Lazard, the author of eleven much acclaimed novels and several short-story collections. The two men had known each other since they were high school classmates on Chicago's North Side. They had been one of the city's best tennis doubles teams over sixty years ago and had remained good friends through the years. Even so, Michael had been reluctant to ask Nat to read his fiction. Michael didn't want to take advantage of his friendship, and he feared that by showing his literary efforts to Nat, he would be putting his friend in an awkward position. If Michael's work evidenced promise, great. Nat would tell him so. But if Michael's writing was crap, he knew that Nat would be placed in the uncomfortable position of gently telling his old friend the disappointing truth. So, after much hesitation, Michael emailed "To Die in Chicago" to Nat for his honest appraisal, hoping that this latest story was better than amateurish.

"You have a real gift for transmitting emotion through narrative," Nat told him after reading the story.

"Really?"

"Really. There's some fine writing here."

"You're not just being nice to an old pal?"

"No, I'm not. Frankly, it's better than I expected."

"For a lawyer, you mean."

"That too, but don't get carried away. Scott Fitzgerald you're not quite yet."

"Seriously, your opinion means a lot to me. Do you think there's a chance of getting my stuff published?"

"One short story—that's tough. But if you can put together a collection of ten or fifteen good stories, a publisher might be interested."

"I have at least ten that are pretty good . . . I think."

"Send them to me, I'll read them and give you my comments. And if they're as good as 'To Die in Chicago,' I'll put you in touch with my agent."

"That's wonderful, Nat. I'm very grateful."

"Don't get too excited. There's no guarantee they'll be interested in doing anything."

"Just submitting my scribbles to a real literary agent is kind of thrilling."

That night Michael stayed up late selecting twelve of his short stories that he would send to Nat. He reviewed them carefully but made only minor revisions. After all, he had already revised the stories many times until he was satisfied. When he finally emailed the stories to Nat, it was 2:00 a.m., and Michael was exhausted. He tried to moderate his expectations, but his imagination quickly overpowered his intentions.

"Please welcome Mr. Michael Bliss, author, I should say, best-selling author, of *Along the Way*, one of my Oprah Best Book Summer Selections."

The studio audience exploded in applause as Michael walked on stage to be interviewed by Oprah.

"Michael Bliss," Oprah said, "yours is a remarkable story. You're seventy-five years old, and until *Along the Way*, your remarkable collection of short stories, was released, you had never published anything."

"That's true, Oprah."

"You were a lawyer."

"Yes, I practiced law in Chicago for over forty years."

"Where did these amazingly moving stories come from,

Michael? The *New York Times* is calling you a modern Chekhov."

"That's most kind. I'm not sure where any of it comes from. I've been kind of thinking about writing these things for years, but you know, I was busy being a lawyer and raising a family. I didn't have a chance to write anything until I retired."

The audience clapped enthusiastically.

Then he was in Los Angeles on the set of the movie version of "To Die in Chicago." Clint Eastwood stepped from behind the camera and sauntered over to Michael sitting in his stage-side chair, "Michael Bliss—Writer" prominently printed on it.

"Michael, remember that we're having lunch with Tom and Meryl. I want to make sure that we've got that final scene just right."

When Michael awoke around dawn, he was so stiff that he could barely get out of his chair. The memory of his dream was evaporating with the early-morning mist, and along with it, he experienced a vague sense of disappointment.

Nat confirmed that he had received Michael's twelve short stories and told Michael that he would get back to him in a few days. Michael was apprehensive about his friend's comments. In the meantime, Michael waited and dreamed about his Nobel acceptance speech.

"Frankly, Mike, I'm kind of astonished. You know that I've taught creative writing at the University of Chicago for twenty years. Most of what I see is unremarkable. But once in a while, I come across some good writing. I believe that at least six of your stories are at that high level."

"I don't know what to say—your opinion means the world to me."

"This is strong writing Mike—personal but universal, moving and subtle. In 'Uncle Leo,' when Leo reunites with his son at the Cubs game, I was misty-eyed—and that doesn't happen often. I wish that you had started writing a long time ago."

"I thought a lot about it, but I never seemed to get to it."

"Well, it's pretty late in the game for you, so don't celebrate yet. But whatever happens, you've written some outstanding stories."

"What now?"

"Now I'm going to send your twelve stories to my big-time agent, the esteemed Sidney J. Resnick. Sid will tell me what he thinks—good or bad. Sidney is a truth-teller—rare in this business."

<hr />

"I like your friend's stories, Nat. I do, but it's not like there's a big market for a first-time seventy-five-year-old former lawyer unless he's writing about juicy, celebrity cases. I'm not saying that Michael Bliss couldn't be the exception, but he'd definitely be a long, long shot."

"You agree that his stuff is good."

"It is—in fact perhaps better than much of what's published today."

"So, what's the problem?"

"Come on, Nat—you've been around for a while. How

many copies do you think will sell? These are small stories—personal, intimate . . . not big, sexy themes. How much
marketing and promotion money is a publisher going to put
behind a first-time, old-guy author? Without a full-court
marketing effort, what are we looking at—three thousand,
four thousand copies at best. And at his age, you can't count
on a second or third printing. Your pal would be happy. He'll
be a published author—wonderful. But the publisher would
probably lose money."

"How about quality? Sid, you know books that were
published even when there wasn't a great likelihood of big
sales. Someone took a chance. Who knew what would happen with *Ulysses*?"

"*Ulysses*! Give me a break, Nat."

"But his writing is good—maybe real good."

"So what! As Jack Kennedy said—'Life isn't fair.'"

"What should I tell him?"

"It pains me to say it, but you might consider telling your
old buddy the truth. And maybe you could talk to him about
self-publishing. I understand that some writers have done
okay going that route."

"Michael views that as sort of a failure. He really doesn't
want to do it."

"Well, if he wants to see his name in print, he just may
have to bite the bullet."

"Sid, Mike Bliss is special to me. We go way back. This
writing thing is a real big deal to him. He wants to leave
something important behind when he's gone—more than
money."

"Who doesn't, but, Nat, only a few very talented

individuals leave anything enduring for the future. You especially know this. It's a very select club. The best we can hope for is maybe that our grandkids remember us after we're gone . . . fondly, we hope."

"Look, I'm not saying that my old friend is that once-in-a-century writer, but his writing is worth preserving. I see, you see, work that isn't nearly as good as Michael's hyped far beyond its real quality."

"I don't deny it."

"So, what if I want to give Michael a hand?"

"What do you mean?

"What would it cost to print four thousand copies of Michael Bliss's short story collection and put some muscle behind a marketing campaign? You know, interviews, critics reviews, ads—all that razzle-dazzle?"

"That's an expensive hand you'd be giving your friend. And I'm not at all sure I can get his stories published even if you cover the costs. When did you become a philanthropist? Unless you've been making a ton of money I don't know about, it would be serious expense for you."

"Run the figures, Sid, and let me know."

"Nat, why are you doing this?"

"First, as I said, he's an old and special friend. Second, his writing is excellent. And third, maybe this collection of short stories will sell a ton, which would make me and a lot of other people happy. You never know."

"No, you don't. Surprises all around."

Sid was right. The cost to print and market Michael's collection of stories was not insubstantial, but Nat would willingly handle it.

Nat called Michael and gave him the marvelous news.

"Nat, this is about the best news I've ever had. I can't wait to tell Janice. I can't wait to tell everyone. I feel like I just won the lottery. I'll never be able to thank you enough."

"Just keep writing. I expect great things from you."

After the phone call, Michael considered his sudden good fortune. Of course, he would need to buy a new wardrobe for the television interviews he'd be doing.

The English Girl

I learned from an old friend, who had known both of us, that Paula had died in London. Although it had been thirty years since our affair, Paula had been a constant presence in my thoughts. The fact that she was no longer in this world seemed impossible.

Paula was English—married to a visiting political science lecturer at UCLA. I was a professor in the same department. We met at a faculty and spouses luncheon. She was pretty—not exactly beautiful but with amazing, big, khaki eyes and long hair of the same color down to her waist. She was tall. I liked her patrician looks and her upper-class English accent. Loved to listen to her talk—sophisticated, worldly, disarmingly candid. That's how she came across to me.

I was an American, and that intrigued Paula. She had never visited the States, so everything was new and interesting, including me. And I paid a lot of attention to her. She had married young before she had the experience of receiving abundant attention from other men. Paula was excited by this new world and by my obvious interest in her. She was into art, and her husband, Clark, was not. I leaped at the opportunity and invited her to a tour of the Los Angeles County Museum of Art.

"Their modern collection is one of the best," I told her.

"I'd love to go. You don't mind taking the time?"

"No, I like to show off our native treasures."

"I hope you don't think that we Brits believe that you're all savages over here."

"Maybe, not all of us."

"You don't look like a savage to me."

"You never know."

So, one rainy, early spring Saturday morning that Paula said reminded her of England, but not as cold, we drove to the museum. I didn't know what Paula was thinking, but my fantasy was that we would forget about art and head directly for a hotel where we would have wild sex. That did not happen. What did was that we had a good time. We talked about art, Los Angeles, England and a good deal about ourselves— our childhoods, school, aspirations, disappointments. We did not talk about Clark or about my wife, Clair. The time passed quickly, and I regretted when our day ended. I liked this woman and shared my feelings with my old friend Dennis.

"It's not just the English thing. She's really nice—bright too."

"Be careful, Sammy. She's married, and by the way, so are you. You want to fuck her is one thing, just don't get super serious."

"All I did was take her to the museum. Nothing is going on."

"Not yet, but I know you."

"I'm not about to run away with her."

"Sammy, you're a romantic. You've always been. It's always a drama with you. A fast fuck won't do. You need to fall in love."

"Oh, come on, Den!"

"I'm just saying, be careful. The way you talk about her, I don't know."

Dennis wasn't all wrong. We had been pals since high school, and he had been witness to two of my more serious relationships. At least that was what I called them. Dennis sarcastically labeled them "Sammy's soul mates." Each burned bright and hot for a while, but like a fire that consumes everything in its path, nothing was left in the end but ashes.

"If you're talking about Sharon, that was a long time ago."

"Sam, that just about broke up your marriage—your family."

"I'm not about to do that again."

"All I'm saying, Sam, is that you got a lot to lose—Clair, two great kids. You want to be one of those sad dads who sees their kids every other Sunday?"

"I appreciate what you're saying, but you're going way overboard. I'm not gonna blow up my marriage for a woman I hardly know."

"Good to hear."

I did kind of listen to Dennis, and although I couldn't get Paula out of my head, I didn't contact her for a couple of weeks. Then, out of the blue, she phoned me at my office.

"I hope I'm not bothering you, Sam, but you did say that your brother worked for an advertising agency, and as I told you, I was a copywriter at a London shop. Would it be an imposition if you could put me in touch with him? Frankly, I've got too much time on my hands, and I thought that perhaps I could work while I'm over here. "

I was so excited to hear from her that I just about promised her a key position at my brother's ad agency.

"Great, great! That sounds like a terrific idea. I'm sure that Josh will be happy to talk to you. I understand that Brit copywriters are all the rage at ad agencies in the States. I bet they'd love to see you."

"Do you really think so? You're a prince to help. I'm so grateful."

I told her that I would call Josh first to let him know about her and that he'd be getting a call from her. And I wondered just how grateful she would be. But I left it at that.

Four days later, Josh called me.

"Where did you find her? She's a gem. Did some fine work for a big London agency. We'll have to pay her as a consultant 'cause she's here on a short-term visa, but frankly, we're lucky to have her. And great looking, too. I owe you, bro."

"Always happy to help."

So, what to do now, I wondered. Then, just like that, Paula phoned me. The gods smiled.

"They couldn't have been nicer, Sam. Your brother was so helpful, and I'm going to start there next week working a couple of days a week till they see how it works out. Look, I really appreciate all that you did. May I take you to lunch tomorrow?"

I almost peed in my pants, but I tried my best to sound cool.

"Well, sure, but you don't owe me anything. Of course, I'd like nothing better than to have lunch with you."

I bet she looks amazing naked, I speculated.

I suggested a restaurant in Beverly Hills where I often went. It was frequented by show-biz types, and I thought that Paula would be impressed by the clientele and because I was known there. I arrived fifteen minutes early and was shown to a much-sought patio table by Oscar, the obsequious maitre d'.

"Wonderful to see you, Mr. Salter. I hope you like this table."

"What's not to like, Oscar? Thanks, it's a great table."

It was especially on this perfect Los Angeles day—warm but not hot with an unusually clear, smogless sky, the sun flashing off the handsome tableware and eggshell-white linen. A cut-glass vase holding a single yellow rose added an elegant touch to the table. All around were beautiful people in what appeared to be earnest conversation. A sense of success—of living well—radiated from every corner. The impression of ascendency, perhaps an illusion. After all, this was show-biz central.

"I'm waiting for a lady, Oscar."

"I'll show her over as soon as she arrives."

Waiting, I felt like a kid on a first date. *Come on, Sammy, you're forty years old. Relax, it's just lunch.* I ordered a glass of wine, and I wondered if Paula would join me in a drink. Then I saw her as Oscar led her across the sun-dappled patio. She was wearing a short skirt, not ultrashort, but high enough to show off her long legs, muscular like a dancer's. A silk blouse accented her breasts. When she greeted me with a perfect smile, contrary to what I had told Dennis, I was ready to run away with her.

"I'm so glad to see you, Sam. What a beautiful restaurant."

"You look great."

"Thank you. I couldn't decide what to wear. I hope this is okay."

It's perfect."

"What are you drinking?"

"Wine—a good Pino Grigio. Would you like a glass?"

"That would be lovely."

"So, tell me how's it going at the ad agency?"

"Well, I've only been there a week—two days, actually. They have me working on the California Tourism account. I'm not sure yet exactly what I'm doing, but it's very exciting."

"I told you that Josh would be thrilled to have you."

"I hope that they feel that way after I'm there a little longer."

"I think that you're going to be just great."

"You know, it's funny, over here you use that word all the time—great; I like it. It's gracious. In England, we seem to use it in a pejorative way—like, he's a great fool."

As she spoke, she touched my arm gently—a natural extension of her conversational style. I liked that.

"Do you miss England?"

"I suppose this will show how shallow I am, but no, I don't miss it. California is so sunny and beautiful. Everybody here looks so tan and healthy."

"I think you fit right in."

She gave me a look that was somewhere between curious and concerned.

"Are you flirting with me, Sam?"

I wasn't sure what to say.

"I guess I am—a little."

"Are you that kind of guy—you know—who flirts with all the women?"

"I haven't done much flirting in some time. You bring out the flirt in me. I hope I haven't offended you."

She looked at me closely and hesitated for perhaps five seconds.

"No, I'm not offended. I'm flattered. I think I like you."

"I like you too."

By the time we finished our Cobb salads and two more glasses of Pino Grigio, I was in trouble—a thrilling, scary, dangerous, illicit trouble. I wasn't sure what to say. When we parted, she kissed me quickly and lightly on the lips.

⸺⸺◦《◉》◦⸺⸺

My three-bedroom, two-bath house in Westwood is modest for the area, but it has a swimming pool in which I floated the Saturday after my lunch with Paula. My mind floated too, back and forth, winding up in the same place—Paula.

"You've been bobbing around the pool for hours. You'll get waterlogged."

It was Clair.

"Just relaxing."

"Enough relaxing. You need to pick up Amy at the Millers'. I'm making dinner."

"I sort of lost track of the time."

"You've been in kind of a trance all afternoon."

"I've just been, you know, thinking."

"About what?"

"The usual—office politics, next quarter's program. That kind of stuff."

"Sometimes, Sam, I think that you're in another world—way out there somewhere."

"Okay, I'm back to the real world. I'll pick up Amy."

"Sooner than later, please."

A week passed. I didn't hear from Paula, and I didn't call her. Maybe our lunch had been a quirk fueled by wine and a false sense of intimacy. Maybe we were both reckless or just horny. I seemed paralyzed—unable or unwilling to follow up. I was afraid of where all this might lead. Best to just let it go, but I couldn't. I phoned Paula at the ad agency.

"Paula, I just wanted to tell you that I really enjoyed our lunch . . ." I hadn't meant to, but I blurted out: "I miss you. I'm sorry. I must sound silly."

"I wanted you to call."

"I think about you all the time. Can you get away—maybe meet somewhere we can be alone?"

"I want to, Sam, but all of this, us, it's too fast. This is new to me. I don't know how to handle it."

"I know it's scary."

"It is. We're married. I don't want to hurt anyone. Sam, I'm not the type to play around."

"I don't have answers. And I don't know where this is leading, maybe nowhere, but we need to at least talk."

"Talk's not what worries me. I have to think. I'll call you tomorrow at your office."

I had known Clair since high school. We married in our early twenties and had our first child, Amy, when I was twenty-five. Our son, Nate, was born three years later. Who knows what you want in a wife when you're young? Some do. I didn't. Clair wanted to get married. She was pretty, funny, smart and persistent. We had loads of friends, most of whom were also getting married. At the time, it seemed like the right thing to do. In the beginning, it was okay. Clair taught third grade while I was working on my doctorate. Our life was busy, our goals mutual. We were moving ahead together. And we got there. Prestigious career for me, exultant motherhood for Clair. Two healthy children for us. A nice house in a good neighborhood and a swimming pool to boot.

I can't pinpoint the specific time when it started to unravel. Maybe when we bought the house in Westwood. That was the last piece of our dream come true. Pop the champagne! Live happily ever after! But somehow I missed the celebration. Was this it? Because if it was, I had a problem. There had to be more. It was enough for Clair, I supposed, but not for me. I wanted a bigger life—more interesting, more exciting, Was this fair to Clair? No. Should I have tried to work together with Clair to achieve that so-called bigger life? Certainly. Did I try? Kind of, but not too diligently. So, by the time I met Paula, our marriage was troubled.

Clark Graham didn't share his wife's affection for Los Angeles. For starters, he hated the eye-straining smog and glaring sunlight, so different from the cold, gray palette of his native island. His eyes were often irritated, and his pale skin burned red rather than tanned. He liked some of his colleagues at UCLA, but their informality vaguely bothered him. He would be glad to return home after his one-year fellowship. Perhaps more discomforting to him was his wife's exuberant embrace of all things American. Lately, there seemed to be a subtle change in their relationship.

"All this friendliness is a bit off-putting, don't you think?" he asked Paula at dinner in their small apartment.

"Don't be such a scold, Clark. They just want us to feel welcome."

"You think all this bonhomie is sincere?

"I do; they're just more outgoing than we're used to. Try to loosen up."

"Loosen up—yes. I've noticed that you seem to have loosened up quite a bit."

"What are you saying?"

"Nothing, really. Maybe I'm jealous that you've adjusted so well."

"If you just give it a chance, I think you'll start to appreciate it here."

"You really think so?"

"Just try."

"Perhaps the trip to Vancouver will give me a new perspective."

"You know that I can't go."

"I didn't expect you were. It's only three days. 'Britain's Rightful Role in the Israeli-Palestinian Conflict.' I make my small contribution on the panel, listen to the brilliant insights of other academics and return to paradise and my loving wife."

"Are you being sarcastic?"

"Not at all. This is paradise, is it not? And you are my loving wife, are you not?"

"Don't be an ass, Clark."

"I don't mean to be."

"When are you leaving?"

"Next Friday morning and I'm back Monday night. I'm sure that you'll manage splendidly without me."

"I'll do my best."

Three days. I've got three days. Paula weighed that thought. *Three days with Sam, if I dare.*

———— ((◊)) ————

The view from my room on the twenty-third floor of the Hyatt Hotel in downtown Los Angeles looked toward the Pacific Ocean some twelve miles west. From this height I observed the noxious yellow-brown smog that hung over the City of Angels like a shroud. I paced across the thick beige carpet embroidered with some kind of blue-and-orange flowers for the tenth time. Would she come? She had said she would.

We had chosen this hotel together. Coconspirators because it was downtown far enough from where we were likely to be recognized. Now we shared a secret. But would she come? The knock at the door jolted me. *My God, she's actually come.*

"I didn't think you would come."

"I wasn't sure I would."

"I'm very glad you're here."

"I don't know what I'm doing, Sam. I don't know if I can do this."

"Look, Paula, if this feels wrong to you, it's okay. We don't have to do anything. It's all right—I'll understand."

"You think I'm so sophisticated, Sam, but I'm not—not about this kind of thing. I'm scared to death."

"For what it's worth, so am I."

"Really?"

"Paula, I'm not going to pretend that my record is unblemished. I've been around the block. I've made mistakes, but believe me, this is different."

"I've never done this. I'm afraid I'll disappoint you."

"You couldn't."

I reached out for her, and she fell into my arms. We kissed gently at first then passionately—her lips, her neck, her hair. I wanted to swallow her. We were pressed tight together. I felt her heart beating fast, her breasts against my chest. Then she stopped, her dazzling eyes unblinking.

"I think it would be best if we got rid of our clothes."

Sex can fuck you up. And if that sex is the best you've ever had—new, uninhibited, with nothing off-limits and all of it deliciously clandestine—it affects your entire life. I was thinking with my dick, if I was thinking at all. But this was more than about great sex—right? Paula and I were soul mates. We were the perfect fit that everyone wants and almost never finds. Complicated, yes—a husband, a wife, two kids, lives already built somewhere else with someone else. What to do about that? Best to not think about it too much right now. What ran through my mind at that moment like a movie playing over and over was our entwined bodies. The scent of her perfume and our mingled sweat was as vivid today as it was thirty years ago.

Adultery is a tricky business, and successful adulterers need to be good actors as well as good liars. Over the next two months, Paula and I performed our parts well, especially Paula, which was a surprise to me. Our weekly assignations were carefully planned. We were discreet. We confided in no one. We were more alive than at any time in our lives. We couldn't get enough of each other. Time loitered between our meetings then rushed when we were together. We didn't talk about the future because we were afraid that it would ruin the present. So we didn't make plans, but we couldn't stop thinking about what might be.

Then, one postcoital afternoon, Paula posed a question.

"So, where do we go from here?"

Seven words that broke the spell. I knew it was coming, but somehow I wasn't quite prepared.

"What do you mean?"

"You know what I mean. Are we having an affair—an

exciting sexual dalliance—or is it something more? I need to know, Sam."

"It's more than an affair."

"Don't be angry at me. I know this complicates things."

"I'm not angry at you. Where do *you* want us to go from here?"

"Would it frighten you if I told you that I loved you?"

"Frightened and happy."

"Do you love me?"

"Yes, and that scares the hell out of me."

"Why?"

"Because we're talking about big stuff here. Life-changing stuff. Are you ready for that?"

"Are you?"

"It won't be easy—there'll be a lot of pain."

"I know, and it makes me ill to think about it. Is it worth it, Sam? I think that's the real question."

"One of the things that I love about you, Paula, is that you get right to the point."

"I have to. I need to know where you stand, Sam. If we're together in this, I think I can handle anything."

"Look, I know that even though we haven't talked about it, we've been thinking about this thing—all the time—so yes, we're together. We want the same thing. I guess we better start to figure out how to get there."

Was I sure? I wanted to show Paula that I was committed—ready to make that monumental leap of faith. In truth, I was in a panic. Was I honestly ready to change my life—make a new future with this fascinating woman I had known for all of three months?

————)(◐)(————

Procrastination and delay followed. The sex was amazing, but now enormous decisions had to be made, so when we weren't in bed, we talked and talked about how to go about changing our lives. In a way, it was simple—end our respective marriages and move on together into a bright and beautiful future that I couldn't quite believe in even though I assured Paula that I did. So, we talked, we plotted and planned but we didn't act. Something outside ourselves would have to happen to end the inertia.

————)(◐)(————

Clair and I were driving back from a small dinner party in Malibu. It was late, and we hadn't said a word to each other. Finally, Clair broke the silence.

"What's going on, Sam?"

"What do you mean?

"You hardly talked tonight at dinner or now."

"I don't know; I've got a lot on my mind."

"You want to tell me about it?"

"There's nothing to tell. I'm just kind of jumpy lately."

"Why?"

"How do I know? Work, money, the kids."

"I don't think so."

"What are you getting at?"

"Stop the bullshit. I know you—how you are when you're

with another woman. Remember, I've been to that movie be-fore—and I can't go through it again. You think I'm a fool—that I haven't noticed what's been going on lately. You're not even good at hiding your little affair. Or is it more than that?"

"I don't know what to say."

"It's the English woman, Paula something, isn't it? I'm not blind. You come home smelling of her perfume and then mope around like a lovesick kid. "

"I'm sorry. I didn't want for it to come out this way. I was going to talk to you—explain things calmly."

"Tell me now then—calmly."

And I did, more or less, calmly. I talked, Clair listened and stared out into the night, at Sunset Boulevard, the pass-ing houses and palm trees, the streetlights casting ominous shadows on the curving road. When I had no more to say, she asked me if I loved "this woman." I said that I thought that I might. Then Clair again calmly told me that she wanted me to move out of the house—that night.

———— ◆◆◆ ————

I spent that sleepless night at the Holiday Inn in Santa Monica. I missed the expected comforts of my house, my everyday routine, my children, my dog. My head ached. My stomach groaned. What was I doing? First thing in the morning I called Paula and told her what had happened the previous night.

"My God, why didn't you tell me you were going to do it?"

"It just came out. I didn't plan it. I thought you'd be happy."

"I am, darling, just surprised and a little terrified. I suppose everyone will know now."

"I suppose so. Are you ready for this, Paula? Because, if you're not, it's okay with me. You can tell Clark that all of this was, you know, a mistake—temporary insanity. I don't want you to feel pushed into making a decision."

"What are you talking about? I want us to be together. It's just so fast that I'm kind of disoriented. It's what we wanted—what we've been talking about. And now it's actually happened. I'm glad. We don't have to sneak around anymore. I better talk to Clark before he learns about us from someone else."

"Are you sure, Paula?

"If you are, I am."

———— ◦(◦)◦ ————

"Paula, do you know what you're doing?"

Clark Graham had just been told by his wife that she loved another man.

"What do you know about Sam Salter? You've known him for a few months. Are you really ready to throw away our life, our marriage? This is insane. I can't believe we're having this conversation."

"It's hard to explain."

"God damn bloody right it is."

"I don't blame you, Clark, for being angry."

"That's a great comfort. Why don't you take some time to consider this? You're not thinking straight. It's not like you."

"Maybe you don't know me as well as you think you do."

"I guess not. You're like another person I don't even know at all. This man, Sam, he's married—he has children. You think he's ready to give all that up for you?"

"I do."

"Just like that. You're a fool, Paula. I'm not going to beg you, but you're making an enormous mistake. Mark my words—if you do this, you're going to get hurt; you'll wind up with nothing."

"You may be right, but I've got to take that chance."

"Unbelievable."

———⊙———

Paula and I found a one-bedroom apartment in Westwood that we rented for $1,200 a month. She insisted on paying half the rent. I told her that it wasn't necessary, but I appreciated her $600 contribution. Because I was paying all of my family's cost of living, money was tight.

For a couple of months, living this way—the two of us risk-takers in a play-it-safe world—was so new and different that it fended off, at least a bit, the nagging sense of guilt that weighed heavily on me. I was not sure what Paula felt. She told me that she was happy, but she required constant reassurance of my love and commitment, which I readily gave her while wondering exactly what the hell I was doing. Sex became complicated. Now that we had escaped our conventional lives, Paula embarked on a no-boundaries exploration of the erotic. She was the instigator, the aggressor. Nothing was off-limits. I matched, or tried to match, her ardor. Every bit of it was electrifying and more than a little exhausting. Something else—there was a desperation in all our sex play, an unspoken fear that we needed this unrestrained passion to hold our shaky lives in place.

<hr />

This was the Sunday that I had Amy and Nate. That was what Clair and I had agreed to. Every other Sunday and every Wednesday night I had the kids. It wasn't a legal agreement. No lawyers were yet involved. Clair and I had worked out our own plan for now. What do you do with an eleven-year-old girl and an eight-year-old boy for a whole day when their world has been turned upside down? They had questions. I offered only evasive answers.

"When are you coming home, Dad?" Amy asked.

"That's hard to say."

"Why?"

"It's kind of complicated."

"Are you and Mom getting divorced?"

"Who told you that?"

"Well, are you?"

"Your mother and I are trying to work things out. We're not the only ones who have problems. I'm sure that you know other kids whose parents have trouble. I don't know exactly what we're going to do."

"Mom says you have a girlfriend," Nate said.

"Look, it's hard to explain. Sometimes moms and dads don't get along. It's not anyone's fault. Your mom and I love you even if we have our problems."

"Are you living with her?" Nate asked.

"Nate, I'm living with her for right now. I don't know if you kids can understand. It's a tough time for everyone—everything is unsettled."

"I don't understand. Do you like her more than Mom?" Amy asked.

"It's not like that. Your mom is a good person. We just don't make each other very happy."

"But your girlfriend makes you happy?" Amy asked.

"You're both too young to understand this kind of stuff. All I can tell you is that your mom and I love you, and we'll always love you whatever happens between your mom and me."

"I don't think that Mom is happy right now, Dad," Amy said.

"I know, and I feel bad about that."

"Is your girlfriend pretty—prettier than Mom?" Nate asked.

"I tell you what. Let's not talk about girlfriends. I don't get to see you much lately, and I miss you. We've got the whole day, so let's have a little fun."

But we didn't. I took them to brunch at a restaurant on the beach in Santa Monica that specialized in wonderful waffles. We had gone there before, and they had loved it. Now they ate little and were reluctant to talk much about anything. It didn't get any better afterward when we spent the remainder of the afternoon on the Santa Monica Pier, another place that they had enjoyed in the past but that seemed to bore them now. I had always had an easy, natural communication with Amy and Nate. This Sunday, everything between us was awkward and strained. When I dropped them at home, they stiffly accepted my hugs and hurried inside, where a silent Clair was waiting.

———— ((●)) ————

Paula and I tried to navigate through our increasingly anxious lives as though our plans were all on course. But they were not. My brother, Josh, told me reluctantly that given the circumstances, he could not continue to employ Paula. So, my talented lover/copywriter was out of a job. I continued my work at UCLA as best I could and carefully avoided contact with Clark Graham. Married friends Clair and I had didn't exactly disown me. They simply kept their distance. The world became Paula and me, and that put massive stress on us. We worked hard to allay the tension. Sometimes it worked, but it required a heavy dose of self-deception, and the process was enervating. Along with a fair measure of guilt that we both felt, there was the practical problem of money. I was paying for all of the expenses of my family plus the costs of Paula's and my new life—minus Paula's now lost contribution from her defunct copywriting job.

"Maybe we should find a cheaper apartment," Paula suggested.

"Where? Not anywhere around here. It's too expensive,

and we'd have to break our lease, which would cost money that we just don't have."

"I'm just trying to be helpful."

"I know. I'm sorry. I don't mean to be dismissive."

"Are you angry at me?"

"No, no, of course not. It's just that right now money is short, and it's got me uptight. I don't mean to take it out on you."

"Sam, I know it's a difficult time. And I know that I'm asking a lot of you. It's just that you're everything that I have. Without you, I'm pretty much alone in a place I don't even know."

"Don't pay any attention to me. I'm just acting like a jerk. We're going to get through this."

"I'm sorry, Sam, to be so needy. I'll get better."

"We'll both get better, believe me."

"I want to believe you."

I wanted to believe me too, but it became harder and harder to convince myself that Paula and I had a rosy future or any future. I showed Paula none of my doubts. Or, at least, I thought that I had concealed them from her. The truth was that both of us were adrift—disconnected from our old familiar lives. And our new lives were not working. We struggled to deny that deeply frightening reality—to remain upbeat, hopeful. We increasingly got on each other's nerves. Her habit of spending hours working tirelessly on complex jigsaw puzzles, which I once found charming, now seemed to me a colossal waste of time. My tendency to complete the dialogue in old movies we watched on television before it was spoken by the actors, which heretofore I was sure impressed Paula, now was viewed by her as vulgar. We often argued.

"We can't ignore it, Sam. We need to talk about it."

It was the fact that Paula's visa was going to expire in less than ninety days. At that time, she would have to leave the United States or be in violation of the law and subject to deportation.

"It's not like we haven't talked about it. It seems like we've talked about nothing but your visa lately."

"Talked more *around* it is more accurate."

"Look, I wish you didn't have this problem—that *you* could just stay."

"I'm sorry—I thought it was *our* problem."

"It is. My mistake. It's our problem. I'm just frustrated because I don't have any good answers."

"I think that you do if you really want me to stay."

"That's not fair."

"What I mean, and what I'm sure you know, is that you would find a way for me to stay if you were sure about us. And what's more obvious to me all the time is that you're not sure—are you?"

"Jesus, Paula, give me a break. I'm getting squeezed here. We need some time without all this pressure."

"Unfortunately, I'm running out of time."

"And that's my fault? I'm sorry; I didn't mean it that way. It's just that I have so much to deal with right now, and this visa thing doesn't help."

"Sam, I'm not asking you to marry me right this minute if that's what you think."

"Maybe you forgot—I'm married, and so are you."

"I haven't forgotten, but thank you for pointing it out."

"Look, Paula, I don't want to fight. I'm sorry that things haven't gone exactly smoothly."

"No, they haven't. I just thought we had something special. Was I wrong?"

"I don't think you're wrong. It's just that there are so many complications—so much pressure and no time to sort it all out. Be honest, are you absolutely sure about us?"

"I don't know. I used to think that I was, but now, I'm not going to lie, I just don't know. I think that I wanted it to work so much that I kind of lost my bearings. Life with you here in California, you know, maybe it was just a foolish dream."

Over the next week, we tried to fix the unfixable, but our hearts weren't in it. We were not angry with each other. There were no recriminations—no threats—just the hollow acknowledgment that we were done. Like one of Paula's jigsaw puzzles, we now strove to put the pieces of our shattered selves into some semblance of our former lives.

It's strange that when the magic escapes from a relationship how very quickly pragmatism takes its place. A remarkably gracious Clark welcomed back a repentant Paula. Clair, after some hesitation, forgave me, and chastened, I resumed my life as husband and father.

After Paula returned to England, I never spoke to her again.

Clarity

In high school, Bucky Leff was an indifferent student; al-though at that time, he would not have possessed the vocabulary to use that adjective. More likely he would have assigned himself a solid C academic grade. In a graduating class of 452, Bucky ranked 220.

The only novel that he had read in full was *The Amboy Dukes*, a best-seller by Irving Shulman, written in 1947, which tells the story of delinquent Jewish teenagers in Brooklyn. Hot stuff to Bucky—a classic. Bucky's real name was Westly, but only his mother addressed him that way. Other than *The Dukes*, Bucky's reading consisted of a thorough daily study of the sports section of the *Chicago Sun-Times*. His only other aesthetic interest was the movies, which he regularly attend-ed. *On the Waterfront*, *Sunset Boulevard* and *Blackboard Jungle* were among his favorites.

So, when he graduated in 1954 from Senn High School on Chicago's North Side, a crisis loomed. University. The problem was not being accepted by the University of Illinois at Urbana-Champaign some 120 miles south of Chicago. In those far less competitive 1950s, the University of Illinois was required to accept any and every Illinois high school graduate into their freshman class. Bucky's concern was not getting in. It was staying in. The U of I was widely known to flunk out a significant percentage of first-year students. As a C student whose study habits were nonexistent, Bucky Leff feared that he would be among those quickly dismissed. Then what? His dad, a hardworking furniture store manager, had agreed to finance young Bucky's higher education, but if he flunked out, all bets were off. The failed student would then be required to find a job, would be on his own. A terrifying thought to an eighteen-year-old who had been taken care of all his life. Bucky also considered the social disgrace of academic failure—of the loser tag he would carry. And what kind of menial job could he expect to land as a university dropout? So, it was a powerful anxiety that gripped young Westly (Bucky) Leff on his first day as a freshman University of Illinois student. To make matters worse, a nasty case of acne had erupted on his almost beardless face.

⇒◦◦◦◦⇐

Steven McIntire was also starting at the University of Illinois at Urbana-Champaign campus. But not as a freshman. McIntire had completed his master's degree in English at the University of Kansas and was now beginning the much-respected U of I doctoral program in American literature. On this crisp, sunny September day, strolling past the bronze alma mater statue in the main quad, twenty-six-year-old

Steven felt good. He was now on the last leg of achieving his goal of earning a PhD in American literature, and then he foresaw a prestigious career as a university professor. He would also be teaching an English course, Rhetoric 101, which all freshmen were required to complete. McIntire had taught a couple of undergraduate courses at Kansas and had enjoyed the experience. He looked forward to the prospect of molding the minds of young men and women and of perhaps being a mentor to some.

The academic life appealed to him. The knowledge imparted by educators, the exactitude of scholarship, the satisfaction of quiet study, the respect in which society held a professor—all of it was a worthy ambition for this son of an Akron, Ohio, factory worker. As multicolored leaves swirled across his path, he headed for his first teaching class with a sense of purpose.

※

The classroom in Lincoln Hall for Rhetoric 101 was completely filled with twenty- six incoming freshmen, one of whom was Bucky Leff. The room was overheated, which may have partly explained the young man's profuse perspiring. He kept drying his face with a by now almost wet handkerchief. He'd been told that the sweat aggravated his acne. The syllabus had described Rhetoric 101 as a course that sought to develop students' writing proficiency. Bucky was pretty sure that of the twenty-six students in this stuffy classroom, he was the most challenged to develop that ability. He slouched into his desk near the back of the classroom and tried to be as inconspicuous as possible.

The teacher introduced himself to the class as Mr. McIntire. He wrote his name in chalk on the blackboard. It made a squeaky sound. Bucky dutifully wrote Mr. McIntire's name in his new notebook. Steven McIntire didn't look much older than most of his students except that he wore a suit and tie and carried a large, worn leather briefcase. McIntire looked around the room through his rimless eyeglasses and addressed the class.

"As you can see, my name is McIntire—Steven McIntire. I prefer that you call me Mr. McIntire, and I will refer to you by your surnames as well. I'll be passing out the course syllabus, which will describe the material that I intend to cover in this mandatory subject. In summary, I would say that the objective of Rhetoric 101 is to teach you to express yourselves clearly in all your writing. As you pursue your education, I think that you will see that these writing skills will be indispensable to your success."

Bucky slumped down farther at his desk and wrote, "Sirname" (sic) in his otherwise unmarked notebook.

It wasn't that Bucky felt he was stupid. As his mother had told him often, he simply had not used his mind. "Westly," she said. "Your brain is like a muscle; you need to use it, or it will waste away."

Now he worried that years of disuse had permanently impaired him. Maybe it was too late to strengthen this lazy organ. What gave him a smidgen of confidence, a bit of hope, was that others he knew who shared his academic mediocrity had somehow succeeded at college. If they could make it, why not him? So, with these conflicted emotions spinning around his struggling mind, young Mr. Leff listened closely to Mr. McIntire explain the first assignment for the students of Rhetoric 101.

"Your first assignment is to tell me why you are at the university, and what you personally expect to accomplish in this class. Clarity is most important, but if there happens to be a unique prose stylist among you, all the better. The assignment is due one week from today and must be at least five hundred words. I prefer typed copy, but I will accept neatly handwritten versions. This task is meant to give me an idea of the present level of your writing ability. I will not grade this initial assignment."

At least he's not going to grade this paper, Bucky thought. Why am I here and what do I expect to accomplish? That didn't seem impossible. He could do it. And even if his effort showed Mr. McIntire that he needed a lot of improvement, wasn't that the goal of the course . . . to teach these skills? But how to start? After his classes, he went to the imposing campus library and found a place occupied by three other students at one of the long oak tables in the main reading room. Mr. McIntire had emphasized clarity, so Bucky thought, I should just write as plainly as possible. He wrote, "I'm here at the U of I because _____." He wasn't quite sure of the answer, so he stopped to think.

After a moment, he crossed out what he had written and wrote, "I want to continue my education and improve my writing through my studies in Rhetoric 101." Bucky looked at those sixteen lonely words surrounded by an otherwise blank page and felt a quiver in his stomach. *That's awful!*

He realized that he had restated the objective that McIntire had said was the purpose of the course. As to his reason for attending the U of I, again, he had simply noted the obvious. Of course he was here to continue his education. So was everyone else. What he had written was clear enough but didn't really tell McIntire anything interesting about himself. He could do better than that. And he had at least another 484 words to better explain himself . . . if he could. *Well, clarity means to be clear. So I need to say clearly and honestly what I expect to learn in this class and at the university.* Honesty, truthfulness. It seemed to him that they were part of clarity. *Maybe I can write about my fears and doubts—explain myself, or try, anyway. What do I have to lose? McIntire is not grading this first assignment.* After several false starts, Bucky finally came up with an opening sentence that he thought reflected his real doubts and anxiety. He read it softly to himself.

"Sometimes I think that I'm just lost."

Over the next week, in addition to his homework in Spanish, biology and economics, Bucky devoted many hours to his Rhetoric 101 assignment. He wrote. He rewrote. He rewrote again. He frequently consulted his *Webster's College Edition Dictionary*, a gift from his dad. When he wasn't sure of the proper grammar or punctuation, which was often, he asked the librarians for help. They patiently provided that assistance. He put it right out there about how frightened he was of failing, of his lack of knowledge, of winding up work-ing at a dead-end job. With every word he wrote, he tried as best he could for truth and clarity. It was difficult to put these feelings into words. He was kind of embarrassed to reveal his secrets. But he was determined to conceal nothing—to be open and honest and, of course, clear. When he was finally finished, he counted the words—614. He hoped it wasn't bad. He knew that he had done his best, and that made him feel for the first time in his life that he might have accomplished something important.

He carefully copied in his best penmanship those 614 words. He wrote them three times until he was satisfied. He titled his paper "Clarity."

After he handed in "Clarity," Bucky was seized with misgiving. McIntire would certainly find his meager effort woefully inadequate—that he had misunderstood the assignment. Waiting the week for Mr. McIntire's comments was agony. He often wished that he could somehow retrieve his paper before McIntire read it. At last the time arrived for the assignments to be returned to the students of Rhetoric 101 with Mr. McIntire's appropriate suggestions. Bucky braced himself for the worst but hoped for some small affirmation.

Mr. McIntire removed the finished assignment papers from his briefcase and set them on his desk.

"I want to thank all of you for your work completing this first assignment. It's clear to me that some of you have given a great deal of thought to the assignment. Others of you, perhaps not so much. I believe that your work has given me a good idea of the level of your present writing abilities, which as you recall, was my objective. Some of you have already developed some basic writing skills. Others have quite a bit to learn. All of you, I am certain, will benefit from this class."

At this point, McIntire paused, adjusted his glasses and set one assignment paper aside from the others.

"Once in a while, in a class like this, a teacher is fortunate to receive a student paper that is far more accomplished than one would expect. Rarely do we see writing approaching the appellation of literature. Today, I'm delighted to say that I have received such a student paper, which I believe all of you will benefit from hearing me read aloud. It is titled 'Clarity.'"

Mr. McIntire then read Bucky Leff's first sentence.

"Sometimes I think that I'm just lost."

War Story

The first time that I learned about death was in 1944, two weeks after my ninth birthday. To be clear, I was aware of death in general. World War II radio reports told of the number of casualties in various battles in far-away lands with strange names like Anzio, Salerno, Bataan and Guadalcanal. At the local movie theater that I attended Saturday afternoons, the Nortown on Western Avenue, news clips showed violent fighting and dying. But I had never experienced death on a personal basis. When John Manning, our neighbor's twenty-year-old son, was killed on the island of Kwajalein, death all at once became much more real.

My family lived in Chicago on the second floor of a three-flat apartment building in Rogers Park. Our apartment, like the other two, consisted of three bedrooms, one bathroom, a kitchen, a dining room and a living room, which was used only for special occasions. Almost all of the apartment buildings in the neighborhood were three and six flats separated by narrow walkways of about six feet. In the summer, that space provided shade from the hot sun and some protection from icy winds in winter. My mother and father, younger brother, Arnie, and my grandmother shared our apartment except that, since 1942, my dad was away serving overseas in the navy.

When I came home after school one frigid Thursday afternoon in February, I knew something unusual was happening. My mom was absorbed in a serious phone conversation and uncharacteristically waved me away when I asked what was going on. When she finished, she looked at me sadly and said, "Poor woman, first a husband and now a son."

"What do you mean, Ma?"

"Howard, you know Mrs. Manning who lives across the alley?"

"Sure, she lives next door to Donny Bederman's family."

"Well, I'm very sad to tell you that her son, John, a marine, was killed a couple of days ago on an island in the Pacific. Her husband passed away just two years ago and now this. It's terrible."

I didn't know what to say, so I just blurted out, "How did John die?"

"I was told a Japanese sniper shot him."

I knew what a sniper was because I had seen a movie that had a sniper in it.

"I'm real sorry, Mom."

"We all are, Howard. I'm afraid Mrs. Manning is alone now. John was her only child."

I hardly knew Mrs. Manning, but I remembered that she always gave me a whole box of Black Crows licorice when I stopped by her place trick-or-treating on Halloween. She was nice to all the tricks-or-treaters, unlike some of our other neighbors. I felt bad for Mrs. Manning, and for the first time,

I worried about my dad fighting the Nazis far away from home. What if something happened to him? But I didn't say anything then to my mom about my feelings.

———— ((•)) ————

My best friend was Ronny Blum, who lived two blocks from our apartment in a building much like ours. We had been friends since kindergarten. Like my dad, Ronny's father was in the military for what was called the duration of the war. Mr. Blum was in the army stationed in Alabama. Ronny knew a lot about the war. Walking to school the next day, I told him about John Manning, expanding a bit on what my mother had told me.

"A sniper got him, Ron. One shot to the head. He never saw it coming."

"The Japs are smart, Howie. Probably hid in a tree. Could have brought him down from three hundred yards."

"Aren't you glad your dad isn't somewhere he could be shot?"

"Sure, but I don't think he likes Alabama. He told my mom it's kind of boring."

"Yeah, but it's better to be bored than dead."

"How about your dad?"

"We don't hear too much from him. A few weeks ago, we got a letter. He's on a ship in the Atlantic Ocean I think near England."

"Well, he doesn't have to worry about snipers on a ship."

"My uncle Eddie says the danger is German submarines.

You don't see their torpedoes until they hit, and then it's too late.

"I see what you mean."

———=◦《◉》◦=———

My mom told me that a bunch of the women on the block were going to go over to Mrs. Manning's apartment to express their condolences.

"What's condolences?" I asked her.

"It just means we're going to say how sorry we are, give her some company, maybe cheer her up."

"What will Mrs. Manning do now?"

"What do you mean?"

"Does she have anybody to be with?"

"I'm not sure. I think she has a sister in Detroit. It's thoughtful of you to be concerned, Howard, but I'm sure that Mrs. Manning will be okay."

"I hope so."

"Are you worried about Mrs. Manning? I don't want you to get upset."

"Do you worry about Dad?"

"Of course, but he tells us not to worry—that they haven't had any trouble on his ship."

"Uncle Eddie says German submarines sink our ships with torpedoes all the time."

"Your uncle Eddie doesn't know what he's talking about. He's a furniture salesman. Don't pay any attention to him. I'm sorry if he scared you."

"I'm not scared, Ma. I was just thinking about Mrs. Manning and her son, John, and it made me think about Dad."

"Your dad is safe, and he hasn't said anything about submarines or torpedoes. He knows how to take care of himself. It's best for all of us to think positively. Howard, I know before long this awful war is going to be over, and your father will come home."

I hoped that my mom was right, but I couldn't stop thinking of John Manning and how he was never coming home. It had been over two years since I had seen my dad. Sometimes I couldn't remember exactly how he looked. I remembered how he would let me sit on his lap in our car while he was driving and let me steer—how he would play catch with me and call me Speedy when I threw the ball fast—Speedy Fisher, he called me. But somehow, I couldn't remember his face. And I wondered if he remembered how I looked, or Mom or Arnie or Grandma. Had he forgotten us?

To express their condolences to Mrs. Manning, the women on the block brought her gifts—mostly something to eat: a cake, cookies, a pie, a box of chocolates. Our neighbor across the street, Mrs. Kaden, offered a bouquet of flowers. Mrs. Copper, who lived at the end of the block and was a teacher, brought a bottle of wine. Even though it was a Sunday and there was no school, kids didn't go. My brother, Arnie, and I stayed home with my grandma, who was very old and seldom left our apartment.

When my mother returned, it was dark and close to dinnertime. I asked her how the condolences had gone.

"Mrs. Manning certainly appreciated all of us coming to visit, and I know she was grateful for our company. The dear thing just chattered away the entire time we were there. I think it was hard for her when we left. I told her to call me whenever she wanted to. And I'll be sure to stay in touch with her."

"What will she do now?"

"I think that she may move to Detroit to live with her sister, who Mrs. Manning told us has a big house and plenty of room for her."

"Did she say anything about her son?"

"Not much. I'm afraid when she talked about him it just made her too sad."

"Arnie doesn't even remember Dad."

"Why do you say that?"

"He told me."

"Well, you have to remember that Arnie was only three when your dad left."

"Sometimes I can't remember either how Dad looks."

"Sweetheart, I know that all this terrible news about Mrs. Manning's son has upset you. That's natural. Sometimes it seems that this dreadful war is all we talk or think about. But you know, lately the news is getting a little better. I feel sure that your dad will be coming home soon. Then we'll all be together again."

I told my mom that I was sure that she was right, but the truth was that I couldn't stop worrying. What if my dad didn't return? What if a torpedo did hit his ship? What would happen to us without Dad? And my anxiety only increased when the father of a girl in my class was badly wounded in the D-Day invasion of France. That battle was the big news. Our RCA console radio crackled with news reports from Gabriel Heatter. We kept the radio on all the time. When I put my hand on the back, the touch was hot. Newsreels showed what looked like thousands of ships firing their huge guns at the Germans on the shore, the sound so thunderous that it seemed to shake my seat in the movie theater. We saw other ships trying to unload troops on the beach. I was excited and afraid at the same time. And I trembled with terror and pride that my dad might be on one of those ships.

The news of the invasion was all over our neighborhood, all over Chicago, all over the United States—I guess all over the world. The United States and our allies, as they were called—England and France and Canada and other countries—landed at a place called Normandy in France. Thousands of ships and thousands of troops, paratroopers too, who jumped from hundreds of planes. I saw the movies of all of it with my friend Ronny at the Nortown.

"Howie, my mom thinks that now the Germans are on the run—that this is the beginning of the end of the war, at least with the Germans. She doesn't know what will happen with the Japs."

"We haven't heard anything from my dad. My mom says that he's not allowed to write us anything about the battle while it's going on. I'm not even sure if he's there, and my mom won't talk about it, but I kind of think he's there at Normandy. I hope he's okay."

"The guy on the radio—the reporter—he said that the

biggest casualties are on the beaches. Your dad's on a big ship far from the beach. Don't worry."

"Right—and he might not even be there."

———————

But he was there—on a ship called an LST that transported troops and equipment. Ronny was right. My dad was far offshore, and his ship had not been damaged. He was safe. The worst injury on his ship was to a sailor who hurt his back loading cargo.

Our family was, of course, relieved, but the war in Europe and in the Pacific went on. As I walked through the neighborhood, I couldn't avoid seeing gold star flags displayed in apartment windows. I spotted four of them. This meant that someone in that gold-star family had been killed in the war. Every time I saw a gold star, I thought about my dad. More than anything in the world, I didn't want my family to get a gold star. Then one warm day in early May 1945, the war in Europe was over.

My mom was handing me the ration book that I'd needed to buy two pounds of ground chuck at Ernie the Butcher's on Devon Avenue when we heard the announcement on the radio.

VE Day, they called it—Victory in Europe—May 8, 1945. Nazi Germany had surrendered unconditionally. A collective roar swept over the neighborhood. American flags suddenly flew from every apartment. Everyone was hugging and shouting about victory. Car horns blared. People, young and old, danced in the streets and alleys, in backyards and playgrounds. Our next-door neighbor, Mrs. Rudd, yelled across the walkway, "It's over; it's over." Everyone was laughing or crying or both.

A couple of months later, after the new president, Harry Truman, ordered a B-29 to drop atomic bombs on the Japanese Islands of Hiroshima and Nagasaki, the Japs gave up. World War II was over.

My dad was coming home.

Mrs. Manning had moved to Detroit to live with her sister.

Four gold-star flags remained in my neighbors' windows.

Old Friends

T he two old men, both about eighty, met for lunch almost every Friday.

They had been doing this for about ten years. At first their restaurant of choice was a deli in Chicago's Lakeview neighborhood, but as a concession to health concerns a couple of years ago, they switched the meeting place to a healthy-menu café in Andersonville, replacing sodium-packed corn beef sandwiches with salubrious egg-white omelets. The men had been friends since they were classmates in elementary school on Chicago's far North Side.

Phil Rothman was the more talkative of the two, always ready with a story or a joke. When there was a rare pause in the conversation, Phil would quickly step in with an appropriate anecdote. Now retired, he had taught various American history courses at De Paul University for twenty-five years and still attracted a small but loyal following to his weekly blog.

"Trump is a showman, Lou."

"I'd call him more of a conman. Phil, I know people in New York who do business with this schmuck. He doesn't even pay his bills. And now he's president of the United States. Can you imagine?"

"You know I didn't vote for the Donald, Lou. I'm just saying he's not your usual politician."

"He's not your usual anything. He's a nutcase and dangerous. Anyway, we need to make a rule. No talking about Trump. I come here to schmooze with my old pal—to hear again how I scored twenty-eight points against Sullivan in my long-gone youth. Politics should be off-limits. It's too aggravating."

This comment came from Lou Springer, retired partner at Miller, Harrison and Springer Attorneys. Lou had been a star athlete. At six foot three, he was an all-city forward on the Senn High School basketball team in the mid-1950s and then played at the University of Illinois. Lately, Lou's health had been troubling.

The young Mexican waiter took their orders, which rarely changed from one week to the next. Vegetarian chili for Phil, yogurt with granola for Lou. Today, however, Lou said he wanted only a glass of skim milk.

"What's with the skim milk, Lou? You're getting skinny," Phil said.

"Oh, my stomach's on the bum again."

"What kind of lunch is that, skim milk? "

"I'll have a big dinner. Right now I'm just not hungry."

After lunch, Phil phoned Lou's sister, Barbara. Phil had known her almost as long as he had known Lou.

"Not to make a big deal, but I just had lunch with Lou, and I'm a little concerned. He looked terrible—gaunt and ate almost nothing. And he was distracted . . . not like the old Lou. Is he okay, Barb?"

"I'm ashamed to tell you, Phil, that I haven't seen my big brother for about a month. Mort and I were on the cruise for a couple of weeks, and we haven't seen Lou since. He looked okay last time I saw him. I'm sure it doesn't help that since Evie passed away, he's alone in the big Glencoe house.

And Lou's no cook, so I'm sure he's not eating right."

"I didn't want to upset you, Barb. I'm probably overreacting."

"Well, this whole business with Tommy has been hard on Lou. It's been a long time since they talked."

"Too long."

"They used to be real pals. But Tommy didn't even say a word to Lou at Evie's funeral. His own mother's funeral."

Tommy was Lou's only child and had been a lawyer at Lou's firm. Everyone assumed that Tommy would be made a partner years ago, but he had not, and finally, an angry and bitter Tommy quit and started his own firm. The relationship between father and son had further deteriorated when Tommy took several substantial clients of Miller, Harrison and Springer to his nascent firm. That was over two years ago, and father and son had not spoken in all that time.

"I think that I'll give Lou a call tomorrow," Phil said.

"What's going on, Lou?" Phil asked the following day.

"What do you mean?"

"Well, you looked terrible yesterday, and you weren't your usual jovial self."

"So now you're a doctor?"

"I have a PhD. Does that count?"

"No. I need a surgeon, not an historian."

"What do you mean—a surgeon?"

"I was going to tell you."

"What?"

"I have a problem. A cancer."

"Jesus, Lou, why didn't you say something?"

"Probably because I didn't want to admit it to myself. I don't know, Phil—this is hard to accept. I've always been healthy—never sick a day. Now I don't know."

"What kind of cancer?"

"Liver."

"What do the doctors tell you?"

"Nothing good. Unfortunately, it's advanced too far."

"Can they operate?"

"There's a top surgeon at Anderson in Houston who looked at my tests, but he tells me that my odds aren't good."

"How about other stuff?"

"Chemo and radiation are possibilities. They might give me a little more time but not a very good time. And to be honest, Phil, I didn't want to prolong the inevitable."

"Lou, we go back seventy years. I don't know what to say."

"Philly, it's okay. I've had a good ride. I'm eighty. Since Evie died, truth is, most of the time I don't know what to do with myself."

"And now?"

"Excuse the gallows humor, but I'd say my plan is to die with a little class, I hope."

"How long are they saying?"

"If I don't do anything except take meds for the pain, maybe three months, maybe longer. Nobody's sure."

"What can I do?"

"Just be the good friend you've always been, Phil. I don't

want to make this a big drama. I'd like to kind of slip away without a lot of fuss."

"Are you afraid, Lou?"

"I certainly don't want a lot of pain and suffering. I'd like some semblance of dignity, if possible. And it kind of pisses me off that I won't be in the game anymore, and sure, I have some regrets. But no, I'm not especially afraid of death. I never was a particularly religious person, Phil. I don't believe in some kind of afterlife—good or bad. I think when you die, that's it. I did my best to be a mensch while I was here, and then I won't be here. End of story—at least my story."

"How about Tommy?"

"Tommy, I'm afraid, is my biggest regret. I don't know what to tell you about Tommy. My only kid and we don't even talk. Nothing—there's nothing there but hate."

"Tommy doesn't hate you, Lou. And I know that you don't hate him."

"Of course I don't hate him, but he sure gives me the impression that he doesn't want anything to do with me."

"Have you tried to talk to him?"

"Believe me, I've tried, but he doesn't want to hear me. I'm the bad guy.

Since Evie died, he allows me to see my grandkids. That's about it."

"Maybe I can help bring the two of you together."

"I appreciate the good thought, Phil, but I don't want Tommy's pity."

"Lou, you may not have another chance."

"It's not my choice, Phil. Look, I don't want to die estranged from my only son; I don't know, maybe it's pride or just plain stubbornness, but Tommy blames me for a lot of shit that was not all my doing. He's said and done a lot of things that hurt me deeply."

"Who cares now, Lou? You'll both regret not reconciling. It's foolish."

"Maybe so, but that's how I feel right now."

———○———

It upset Tommy Springer each time his father picked up his two boys for one of their outings, as his father called them. He made sure that he was never at his Lincoln Park home when Lou Springer arrived. He delegated the handoff to his wife, Wendy.

"Really, Tommy, this is embarrassing."

"I don't want to get into an argument with him. It's better we don't see each other."

"He's your father, Tom. The only one you have. How long is this going to go on?"

"Come on, Wendy. Maybe you forgot how I worked my ass off all those years to make partner. I never asked for any favors 'cause I was his son. I did a damn good job too, and you know what I got from him—bubkes, nothing except vague promises of a partnership . . . somewhere down line. It's just not something that I can let go."

"I'm not saying your father was right, Tommy. I'm just saying, enough already. Time for both of you to move on.'"

"It's not that easy. "

———⟩«⟨⦿⟩»⟨———

Lou Springer slowly climbed the ten stairs that led to the polished oak door of his son's handsome three-story townhouse. When he reached the door, he was panting and had to rest a minute to catch his breath before he rang the doorbell. He didn't want to look worn out.

"Hi, Wendy. You're looking great as always. I talked to the boys about the architectural river tour. They seemed to be okay with it, so I'll take them off your hands for the afternoon."

"Thanks, Lou. That sounds like a nice plan for a Saturday afternoon. Would you like to come in?"

"That's okay. I'll wait right here for the boys."

"They'll be down right away."

Shaun was fourteen and big for his age. His large feet and hands seemed to belong to an adult. Lee, at eleven, had his mother's thick red hair, as well as her freckles.

"Okay, guys, let's get to the ship."

———⟩«⟨⦿⟩»⟨———

Later that night at dinner, the boys were eager to tell their parents about their excursion.

"It was pretty cool," Lee said. "This guy, the guide, told us all this stuff about the river and the killer buildings along the shore. He knew his stuff."

Shaun interjected, "I didn't know that engineers actually

reversed the river's direction. It naturally flows into Lake Michigan, but they figured out how to make it run the other way. Amazing!"

"Sounds like you all had a good time," Wendy said.

"Absolutely, we did, Mom. It was way better than I figured. Don't you think, Shaun?"

"A whole lot better than the zoo where grandpa has taken us about a hundred times. It was fun when we were little, but the polar bears just don't do it for me anymore."

"Do you think your grandfather had a good time?" Wendy asked.

"I think so, but he was real tired. He actually fell asleep on the boat. I mean, not just dozing. He was out like a light. It was hard to wake him up," Shaun answered.

"Hold on, son—you're saying your grandfather couldn't wake up?" Tommy asked.

"I was kind of scared, Dad," Lee said.

"I think Grandpa's sick. He walks bent over and real slow," Shaun added.

"Well, he's not a kid, boys. I'll check it out," Tommy said.

"I think you should, Dad," Shaun said.

After the boys left the table, Wendy poured herself a generous glass of chilled Chablis.

"Would you like a glass, Tommy?

"Yeah, I think so."

"Tom you need to talk to your dad—and you need to do it now. "

"You might be right, but it could be a lot of things."

"If you're not going to talk to your dad, at least talk to Phil. He'd know."

"I'm not saying I'm not going to talk to my father, as-suming that he'd even answer my call. But if I ask him what's wrong, I won't get a straight answer. He'll just shine me on—tell me he's fine, just tired, which might be true. But you're right; Phil will know if it's something else."

Early the next morning, Tommy phoned Phil.

"Tommy, I'm glad that you called me, partly because your dad specifically told me not to call you. But you're calling me, so I don't think that I'm breaking a confidence by responding to you."

"Phil, you sound like a lawyer. So, what's going on? My kids tell me that my dad's in bad shape—very tired, not himself."

"There's no other way to say this, Tom. He's dying."

There was no response—only silence.

"Tommy, are you there?"

"I'm here—just shocked and kind of numb. You said, dying?"

"He has advanced liver cancer. The prognosis is that he has maybe six months, tops. Tommy, I'm so sorry. I figured your dad would live forever."

"Me too. My God! Six months. There's nothing they can do?"

"Your dad said that's what the doctors told him."

"How is he dealing with this?"

"He seems okay—generally."

"We haven't talked in two years."

"I know—and so does your dad."

"I just never thought about my father dying, Phil. To me, he always seemed indestructible."

"I know."

"We got into this rut where we were both so angry with each other, and it just got worse—two years. Look, Phil, I don't want my dad to die this way—with us not having any contact, no connection. But I don't know what to do. He can be a real hard-ass, and he thinks that I'm completely in the wrong—that all our troubles are my fault."

"Tommy, I'll tell you the same thing I told your dad. It doesn't matter who is right or wrong. Time's running out. It's too late for blame. I remember all those years when you were super close. You did everything together. You guys must have gone to a hundred Cubs games, and I remember Lou staying up all night helping you study for the bar exam."

"I haven't forgotten, Phil. I want to see him—make it right between us. I'd call him, but I'm afraid he wouldn't talk to me."

"Maybe there's a better way. Your dad asked me if I would drive him out to your mother's grave this Sunday. He doesn't think that he's up to making the drive himself. Would you be willing to meet him at the cemetery?"

"You wouldn't tell him that I'd be there?"

"Knowing your dad, I don't want to take the risk that he might pass on the whole idea if he knew that you would be there."

"When he sees me, you know that he could just walk away."

"I don't think that he will."

"I hope that you're right. Anyway, I'll be there, whatever happens."

⊸⟨◈⟩⊷

This early-fall Sunday showed Chicago at its best. The manicured lawns at the cemetery seemed to stretch as far as one could see—the grass still a rich dark green and the leaves on the maple and ash trees just starting to turn a myriad of colors. Sweater weather on this almost cloudless day. A cool breeze barely rustled flowers strewn on some graves. Far more grave stones than visitors.

Tommy was already at his mother's grave. Lou saw him but turned to Phil.

"Was this your idea, Phil?"

"Yes."

"But you didn't tell me."

"No."

"Why not?"

"I wasn't sure you would come if you knew Tommy would be here."

"But you told Tommy."

"I did."

"Because?"

"Because he's just a little bit less of a stubborn ass than you. Would you have come, Lou?"

"I'm not sure."

"Well, anyway, you're both here now, so I'm going to leave the two of you alone to talk . . . or whatever."

For the first time since he had discovered Tommy at the cemetery, Lou addressed his son directly.

"And you're okay with this, Tommy?"

"I'm okay with it, Dad."

"May I ask why so after two years of silence?"

"Look, Dad, I'm not going to pretend that I don't know about your trouble.

The kids told me you were in bad shape when you took them on the boat.

And Phil gave me the details."

"Is that why you're here—pity?"

"No, Dad."

"I think that you both have a lot to discuss, so I'll wait for you in the car,"

Phil offered.

Neither Lou nor Tommy did or said anything to stop Phil from leaving. Now father and son looked apprehensively at each other across the rose-hued gravestone of Evelyn Grace Springer as the evening faded to dusk.

The father spoke first.

"In the last couple of years, I've thought a hundred times about what I would say if we ever got together. Now I don't know what to say."

"I never wanted it to get to the point that we had zero relationship. I always figured that we'd patch things up, but somehow it got worse. I'm not sure why."

"I guess you could say that it's complicated. To put it bluntly, I guess you felt that I had screwed you. Maybe a nicer word is betrayed."

"Something like that. You know, Dad, I always counted

on you to be there for me. Then it seemed like you abandoned me when I needed you most. I worked hard to make partner. I think I earned it. What happened, Dad?"

"You think that I didn't speak up for you? I did. I fought hard, but I'm only one partner. There were some who didn't think that you were ready.

Maybe some didn't like me. We had some fierce battles. In the end, I lost ...

You lost."

"Why didn't you tell me what was going on?"

"Maybe I should have, but what good would it have done? Pissed you off even more. Split up the firm, which, as it turned out, happened anyway."

"At least I would have known that you were with me, Dad."

"Son, I thought that you would know that."

"I was so disappointed, so angry. I blamed you for everything."

"I could ask you the same question. Why didn't you talk to me? We used to talk about everything."

"I don't know. Now it's clear that not talking to you was a big mistake, but back then, I was too hurt and mad to think straight."

"So instead of coming to me, you grabbed a bunch of clients and went your own way. How did you think that made me feel?"

"The honest answer is that right then I didn't care. I just wanted to get even."

"Tommy, when you jumped ship, that really hurt. And I'm not just talking about the money. I mean, my only son just ups and leaves without a word to his father, starts his own firm. I looked like a schmuck. Talk about betrayed."

"I understand it now, Dad, but at that time, I wanted to show you and everybody that they were wrong about me."

"Tommy, we've wasted two years. I've missed you. We used to be a big part of each other's life."

"I'd like to get back to that, Dad."

"Well, I think that it's a good time to start."

As the day's last light slipped away, father and son walked surprisingly briskly to tell Phil the good news.

Mr. Ted

When I worked for Martin Brooks in the '70s, he was the top dog at the big advertising agency where I was a just-hired junior copywriter. Marty Brooks was a rainmaker—a new business superstar who was responsible for bringing over $50 million of billing into the agency. On those few occasions when I saw him, he radiated success in his bespoke pin-striped suit by way of London. Even in the sunless Chicago winter, a salutary tan enhanced his rather ordinary facial features. Was he liked? Probably more admired and maybe envied. He certainly wasn't one of those tyrannical jerks everyone hates and fears. What Martin T. (for Theodore) Brooks was was smart, powerful and rich. I wouldn't say that he was especially friendly around the office, but he wasn't imperious either. He was polite to everyone, even to a twenty-three-year-old novice like me. And what especially impressed me was that Martin Brooks was just twelve years older than me.

Brooks hadn't always been the golden boy. He grew up in the then-emerging middle-class neighborhood of East Rogers Park on Chicago's far North Side. His father worked in the distribution department of the *Chicago Tribune*. Marty matriculated through Chicago's public schools and graduated, like me, from the University of Illinois at Urbana-Champaign. He noted disarmingly that he had been a solid B-minus student.

I said that Martin Brooks was rich, but the money wasn't all from his success in the advertising business. The really big-time money came from his wife, Patty, nee Carlson. The Carlsons were old money, and it would be fair to say that a good part of Marty Brooks's success in landing new business had to do with the Carlson family connections. Don't get me wrong. Brooks was no dilettante. He worked hard, and he knew his stuff. But the family's prominence didn't hurt.

In the ten years that I spent at the agency, Marty Brooks's rise continued straight up. By the time he was forty, Martin T. Brooks was the president of an international advertising powerhouse with offices in cities around the world. I'd often see him interviewed on television, and he and Patty were regulars in the Chicago society and charity scenes. There was even serious talk about him running for the United States Senate.

I can't say that Marty was exactly a mentor to me. I was too far down on the corporate ladder for that, but he kept track of my progress, and, I learned later, he more than once put in an influential word for me. By the time I left the agency to start my own firm, along with two other associates, I was the vice president and creative director of the Chicago office.

As smart as Marty was, he was a moron when it came to women. And the women he got involved with weren't classy types or too bright. I didn't understand why Marty played around. He had a good-looking, influential, seemingly loving wife waiting for him at home. He wasn't even discreet about his dalliances. So, of course, Marty's proclivities regarding the ladies were well-known around town. Inevitably, word got back to Patty and to the Carlson clan, and that was it. The divorce was public and ugly and marked the beginning of Marty's steep fall. The Carlsons made it clear that they had cut all ties to and support for their adulterous ex-son-in-law. Marty hung on at the agency for a while, but without the clout of the Carlsons, he seemed to lose interest and confidence. The rainmaker wasn't making rain. Rumor had it that he was drinking and maybe using drugs too. He would miss days of work at a time. His whereabouts were often unknown. Six months after the divorce, Marty was fired.

That , in a nutshell, was the story I understood of the decline and fall of Martin Brooks.

The years rolled by, and I didn't think much about Marty. I was busy building my business and raising a family, and Marty seemed to have disappeared. Some said that he had moved to Florida. Then one frigid January afternoon, I was checking out an apartment in the Lakeview neighborhood on Oakdale just off Sheridan Road as a possible new home for my recently widowed mother. I had persuaded her to sell the too-big house in Highland Park and to move into a nice two-bedroom in the city close to me and my sister. I called the number listed in the ad and made an appointment to visit the apartment at four. I got there a little early and looked around.

The building was one of those spacious six-flats built in

the '20s. It was well maintained, close to public transporta-
tion, on a first floor so that Mom wouldn't have a lot of stairs
to climb and, especially important to her, pets were permit-
ted, so her much-beloved toy poodle, Ziggy, was welcome.

I was buzzed into the tidy, chlorine-scented marble vesti-
bule by a short, middle-aged man in work clothes.

"Are you the manager?" I asked.

"No, I'm Angel, the janitor. The boss, Mr. Ted, is in the
apartment. I show you."

Mr. Ted's back was to me when I walked through the
open door of apartment 1A.

He was talking on his cell phone.

"I'm meeting the plumber first thing in the morning. It's
not a big job—don't worry. I'll call you afterward. Gotta go.
I'm showing 1A right now."

Mr. Ted was Marty Brooks. I knew it the moment that
he turned toward me. He was mostly bald now, and what
hair he had left was completely gray and a bit long in the
back. His bespoke British suit was now replaced by shape-
less, brown corduroy pants and a bulky Chicago Cubs sweat-
shirt. In that instant, I knew that Marty recognized me too.

"Danny—Danny Korman. My God, I haven't seen you
in—what is it—fifteen years, maybe more. I knew it was you
right away. It's me, Marty Brooks."

"I know. I knew right away too. How are you?"

"Well, you see I'm no longer in the ad biz."

"I knew that, but you kind of vanished. Where have you
been all this time?"

"Nowhere. I've been right here in Chicago." Marty
paused and smiled. "Just not quite as prominent as in the old

days. Anyway, tell me about you. Are you looking to rent an apartment?"

"No—well, yes, but not for me. For my mother. My dad died, and she doesn't need the big house. And I don't live too far. I've got a place in Lincoln Park."

"Great—well, let me show you around while we catch up. It's been a long time."

As Marty led me around the apartment, he pointed out the vintage hardwood floors and wainscoting as well as the recently remodeled bathrooms, the kitchen and the new windows. His understated presentation was effective. I was sure that my mother would like the apartment.

"What's with the Ted?" I asked.

"It's my middle name. I've been using it for years now—Ted Brooks."

"What happened to Marty?"

"The name or the man?"

"What I mean is what's been going on with you all this time?"

"You want the long story or the short version?"

"After all these years, I'll take the long one."

"Okay, but first I'd like to congratulate you. I kind of keep track of what's going on, and I see that you've put together a successful agency. It's a tough business, and you've done well. I knew you would."

"Thanks, I work with a lot of smart people. So, tell me about Marty—Ted—Brooks."

"For old times, just call me Marty. Anyway, it's cold in here. Let me get some heat going. You can tell your mom that there's nothing better than an old water-heating system as long as it's in good shape, and in this building, it is. But there's no place to sit here except on the floor, and I'm getting too old for that. I live in 2B. It'll be easier to talk there."

Apartment 2B was like 1A in its configuration except that it faced south rather than north and was on the second floor. The furnishings were contemporary and minimalist— nothing overdone, everything quite tasteful clean and very neat.

Marty offered me a spartan-looking metal chair that turned out to be surprisingly comfortable when I settled into it.

"Can I get you a drink? Soft or hard, your choice."

"The rumor used to be that you were a big scotch drinker."

"I still like my single malt scotch. How about a Glenlivet?"

"A wee one on the rocks would be great."

Marty returned from the kitchen with two half-filled glasses of Glenlivet with ice and settled into the mauve sofa opposite me. He toasted.

"To old times, Danny. I'm really glad to see you."

"Likewise."

It was strange after all the years sitting here in this chic, tidy apartment on Oakdale Avenue talking to my old boss who now was what? A building manager? Owner? I sipped my scotch.

Outside it had started to snow, the flakes piling up softly on the window ledge outside. I was comfortable. The combination of the Glenlivet and the efficient heating system gave me a warm, pleasant glow.

"Well, after the divorce, I kind of fell apart. I couldn't seem to concentrate. I don't know—I wasn't sure exactly who

I was. Patty and the Carlsons came down on me real hard. They're a tough lot. They just wanted to erase the fact that I had even been part of their family."

"Why didn't you go somewhere else? A bunch of agencies would have been happy to have hired you. Marty, you were a star."

"I just lost focus—a sense of myself. And to be honest, I wasn't at all sure that I even wanted to stay in the business."

"I gotta tell you, Marty. I looked up to you. We all did."

"You're kind to say so, but honestly, Danny, what did you know about me? That I was a hotshot. That I was making a pile of money."

"Yeah, what's wrong with that?"

"I don't know how real it was. It was like I was playing a part and I got good at it. And about the money—by the time the Carlsons and the lawyers got through with me ... Well, I'll put it this way: I wasn't broke, but I sure as hell wasn't rich anymore."

"I don't understand why the Carlsons wanted to destroy you. You weren't the first guy who ever cheated on his wife."

"It's complicated." Marty freshened our drinks. I didn't object.

"So, what are you doing now?"

"I could tell you that I'm in real estate. That sounds like I could be a developer or owner or investor. But the truth is I manage this building and two others like it in the neighborhood. I've done this for the last ten years. Before that, I sold laboratory equipment. My sales territory was Illinois and Indiana. It was okay, but I like this setup a lot more. Driving all around Illinois and Indiana can be a real drag. Anyway, tell me about you, Danny. Are you married? Have a family?"

"I've got the whole nine yards—wife, two boys, a hefty mortgage. How about you? Are you married?"

"Well, I've got a friend. We live here together."

Marty took a gulp of his scotch and studied me.

"I'm gay, Danny. Paul and I have been together now for over seven years."

I stared back at Marty for a moment, not sure of what to say. "I had no idea. You were always screwing around with some broad. I thought that's why your marriage broke up. I don't get it."

"It was all an act, man. Since high school, I knew that I didn't like women the same way that other guys did. But back then, I couldn't go there. Couldn't admit it to myself and certainly not tell anyone else. It was like being a freak."

"Marty, that must have been a heavy load to carry."

"You feel like you have this terrible secret that you have to keep. You're desperate for a way out. I guess that marrying Patty was my way out. That it would make me a normal guy. Big time self-deceit, of course, but I grabbed it."

"I take it that that didn't work."

"The marriage was a disaster. I think that she knew before too long that I wasn't what she thought I was."

"Forgive me for asking, Marty, but didn't Patty suspect something was wrong when you were dating . . . You know, before the wedding?"

"Remember the times. Patty was a virgin. She thought that I was a real gentleman for not pushing her—you know, sexually."

"What was it like with all of your bimbos? Everyone thought that you couldn't keep your dick in your pants."

"The funny thing was that I was trying desperately to

be straight—a macho man with these ladies. That too was a disaster."

"But the Carlsons bought the story that you were a whore hound. Isn't that why they broke up the marriage and brought you down?"

"No, they weren't fooled for a minute. Old Man Carlson and his daughter were real close. Maybe after a year of my being a limp dick, Patty figured out what I was, and she told her father. He confronted me. Scared the shit out of me. He didn't shout. Just told me firmly, very emphatically, that no faggot would ever be married to his daughter. He said that I sickened him. That's the word he used, *sickened*. Told me I should see a psychiatrist."

"You don't have to answer this, but when did you, like, get involved with men?"

"You mean, when did I get it on with a man?"

"Yeah."

"Ironically, not till after the divorce and my subsequent fall from grace."

"How is your life now?"

"Pretty good. I don't have to pretend anymore. And the times are different now. People are more accepting. I got someone I love and who loves me. I don't think about it much, but I'd say that I'm content."

"I'm happy for you Marty."

It was snowing harder now, the wind blasting the snow-flakes in staccato bursts against the new windows of apartment 2B. It was getting late, and I had consumed too much Glenlivet. I would have to be careful driving the few stormy miles to my home and family in Lincoln Park.

Delayed in Salt Lake City

Alan's Version

I'm seventy-six years old now, and I think a lot about the past. About what if I had done this instead of that—taken that road rather than another. I know that it's pointless, but much of what someone does in a lifetime, when you look back, seems arbitrary. The thing is you kind of stumble into life without too much conscious thought, and, *boom*, your whole life is changed big time.

My first marriage was like that. I met Sally when we were both in high school. I had a pretty bad case of acne and found it hard to talk to girls. Sally was a talker. She filled in all the awkward silences and gave me the impression that I could carry on a decent conversation, but she really did almost all the talking. We went together throughout high school and university. There were some interruptions along the way, but mostly we stayed together. We fought often and dated a few others, but we always seemed to reunite. Why? I don't know; maybe it was simply easier than breaking up. Sally was pretty with big, violet eyes like Elizabeth Taylor. Like all teenage boys, I thought constantly about sex—wild, uninhibited, and dirty. Sally provided none of that, but we did kiss and paw each other vigorously. In the 1950s, that was about it sex-wise, and I considered myself lucky. Good girls stayed virgins until they married in that not-yet-emancipated time. I thought that when we married, the sex would be fantastic, and when it wasn't, I felt deceived.

I didn't know how to make it better. My guess is that Sally was disappointed too, but we couldn't talk about it.

Most of all, Sally was crazy about me. Crazy was exactly what she was in other ways. She was like a terribly spoiled child. If she didn't get her way, she'd throw a fit. I'm talking, fall on the floor screaming and kicking. So, I can't say that I wasn't warned. I could have made my escape way back then. But I didn't until about a quarter century and three kids later. So again, I ask myself, why didn't I see this wreck coming? The answer: I did. Next obvious question: If I knew that this relationship was likely going to be big trouble, why did I hang around? I have a bunch of reasons, none that make me look good. Like I was very young, inexperienced and naive. Or I didn't want to hurt Sally . Or I simply didn't know myself or what I wanted in life. Maybe all of the above. Anyway, it doesn't matter. What does is that I stayed and that over the next twenty-five years Sally and I did a good job of diminishing each other.

To be fair, there were some good times along the way. For years, our kids were a shared source of joy. The funny thing is that for someone who was a talker, Sally and I didn't talk much. At least I didn't. Plenty of yelling but not honest communication. It wasn't all Sally's fault. The truth is that not long into our marriage, I pretty much gave up. I didn't know how to cope with this crazy lady, so I went my own way. As individuals, Sally and I were good. We gave and received friendship with others. But just as some relationships are synergistic, ours was destructive. Together, we were less than we were apart.

The 1959 Renault Dauphine was a terrible car. Cute but a real piece of tin. It did, however, have four doors, which is why Sally liked it. My choice was the two-door VW Beetle, a fine automobile then as now. I acquiesced to Sally. We bought the French clunker, setting a bad precedent right at the start of our marriage.

The wedding was in Los Angeles where Sally's folks lived. The plan was that after the ceremony we would drive the recently purchased but fragile Dauphine cross-country to Chicago, where we had grown up, to start our married life. The overpacked Dauphine broke down in Salt Lake City, and it was there that Sally and I had our first big fight as a married couple. It set the tone for the next quarter century.

In 1959 there was no Renault automobile dealership in Salt Lake City, so we looked up *auto repair* in the Yellow Pages and sputtered into Brothers Expert Auto Repair. Their prominent sign noted, *We Guarantee Our Work Since 1946.*

By this time, Sally wasn't yet at her boiling point but was moving quickly in that direction.

"What do they know about fixing foreign cars?

"Sally, they're supposed to be good, and anyway, there's no Renault dealership in this city."

"What if they can't fix it—what then?"

"Well, let's have them take a look at the car and tell us what they think. Maybe it's something minor."

"It's a new car. We just paid $1,600 for it. Now we're stuck here in the middle of nowhere—Hicksville."

"Salt Lake isn't the middle of nowhere. It's a big city."

"With no Renault dealer. Great."

"Look, the place looks pretty substantial. The building is big and clean. It looks very professional. And they're busy. That tells us something."

"Alan, since when are you an authority on car mechanics? What you know is how to fill up the gas tank, and that's about it."

Our conversation was interrupted by the approach of a tall man dressed in green overalls and a spotless white shirt embroidered with the name Hank.

"What seems to be the trouble?"

"A warning light came on between here and Las Vegas. Said it was overheating," I answered.

"I can't say that we're experts in French cars, but we can certainly take a look."

Sally jumped in. "If you don't know anything about these cars, what good are you to us?"

Hank looked a little stunned but smiled.

"Ma'am, I said we weren't experts. I expect if it's like cars everywhere, we'll be able to tell you what the problem is. Of course, you can take your car somewhere else, if you like."

Sally stared at Hank.

"Oh, go ahead and check it out. But we don't want to hang round here forever."

"We're busy, but I'll get a couple of my best men on it

right away. You're welcome to wait in our customer lounge. There's a TV."

"How long will we have to wait?" Sally demanded.

"I can't say for sure, but I know you're in a hurry, so I'll try to move it right along."

Hank then carefully drove the Dauphine into one of the repair bays, and we headed for the lounge.

"He seems very professional."

"Give me a break, Alan. We don't have a choice. We're stuck with these guys."

We shared the customer lounge with four others all patiently watching *Gunsmoke* on the black-and-white television set. Sally loudly complained about Salt Lake City, France, Renault, Brothers Expert Auto Repair, *Gunsmoke* and especially me.

After an hour that seemed longer, Hank returned.

"Nothing major. You need a new alternator. That's not a big deal. The only thing is we'll have to order the part from Renault in LA. They told us they can have it to us in two days."

"Two days," Sally screamed. "We can't wait two days in this dump."

"Take it easy, ma'am. There's no need to raise your voice. You need a new alternator, and the nearest one is in Los Angeles. As soon as we get it, we'll right away install it, and you can be on your way."

The other customers in the lounge were trying hard to pretend that they weren't there. They stared at the television, seemingly transfixed by Marshal Dillon.

I thought that it would be a good time to say something.

"Hank, setting aside the two day wait, what do you figure this will cost?"

"The alternator is $140. Labor may be three hours—say $150. Altogether under $300."

"God damnit!" Sally burst out. "You better do something about this, Alan. I'm not sitting round here for two miserable days. And I'm not paying $300. That's outrageous."

By now the other lounge customers were moving as inconspicuously as possible toward the door.

"Take it easy, Sally," I said, trying to placate her. "We're not in a race to get to Chicago, and the cost doesn't seem too bad. We can take it easy for a couple of days—look around the town."

"What's wrong with you, Alan? Are you a complete idiot? I'm not gonna hang round here for two days, if it really is only two days. And if you're too stupid to know you're getting taken, I'm not."

"Frankly, ma'am, I don't care if you have us do the job or not. But maybe you should listen to your husband," Hank said.

"Why don't you mind your own business," Sally hissed at Hank.

"I'm trying to—believe me. Look, I'm gonna leave you alone. You two decide what you want to do and let me know."

Hank left us in the customer lounge—just the two of us now and Marshal Dillon and his sidekick Chester flickering on the TV.

As soon as we were alone, Sally started screaming at me.

"I'm your wife, and you're on this Hank asshole's side."

"Instead of yelling like a spoiled kid, why don't you shut

up for a minute and think? What the hell do you expect me to do, fix the car myself? Maybe you forgot it was your idea to buy this piece of crap in the first place."

Now Sally was crying, tears running down her cheeks and snot oozing from her nose and trickling onto her upper lip.

"I hate you, Alan. What good are you? You get us stuck in this hellhole, and all you can do is blame me."

"I'm not blaming you. I'm just trying to get you to be reasonable. It's not a catastrophe. We can check into a nice hotel for a couple of days. By then the car will be fixed, and we'll be on our way to Chicago. It's not that big a deal."

"This place, these people—they give me the creeps. I want to get out of here now—not in two days. Can't you understand?"

"For Christ's sake, grow up. We got a busted car. It's gonna take a couple of days to fix. It's not the end of the world. You got a better plan?"

"If you're so smart, tell me how we're gonna pay for all this—the car and the hotel."

"We've got enough."

"It'll take all our money. We won't have anything left. We're gonna be trapped in this miserable dump with no money."

"What's wrong with you? It's two days we're talking about. I'm telling you—we have enough money to get us to Chicago, and then I can borrow some money from my parents."

"Your parents don't even like me."

"Where did that come from? They like you fine."

"No, they don't. I know they didn't want you to marry me."

"What are you talking about? They've never said one word to me about my not marrying you."

"They never talk to me."

"That's how they are. They don't talk to me much either. It's a generational thing."

"I don't even care. All I want to do is get out of here and get to Chicago."

"So do I, but I don't have a magic wand that I can wave, and, *zip*, we're in Chicago."

"I'm not staying here for two days. I can't. I won't."

"There's no other choice unless you have a better solution."

"Why can't we fly to Chicago? You can come back for the care later."

"Are you crazy? That makes no sense. Two little days— that's all it is. Grow up!"

"Two days, and it'll probably be more, in this horrible place, and I'll go crazy."

"Really? You're already crazy. Just think for a second. We fly to Chicago, and I fly back to pick up the car. That's the dumbest thing I ever heard. You're being impossible."

"I am not. You're the one who won't even listen to me."

"I'm not gonna listen to a lunatic. We are not flying to Chicago. We're gonna wait two days till the car is fixed, and then we'll drive to Chicago. It's not a tragedy. It's only two days and three hundred bucks. You'll just have to live with that."

Now, in addition to the flowing tears and snot, Sally's face was crimson, and her entire body was shaking.

"Go to hell, you son of a bitch. I'm not your slave. I'm not gonna do what you say just 'cause you say it. If you won't fly with me to Chicago, I'll go myself."

And that's what Sally did. She got her suitcase out of the Dauphine, took a taxi to the Salt Lake City airport and flew to Chicago.

I stayed in Salt Lake City for two days until the car was repaired and then drove alone to Chicago.

I've tried to remember if I considered getting out of the marriage at that time. I don't recall what I thought about as I drove those solitary highways through Utah, Wyoming, Nebraska, Iowa and finally to Chicago. I got ahold of Sally when I phoned her from Omaha at her brother's apartment in Chicago. She said that she was sorry, and I said that I was too.

Sally's Version

I liked Alan. Everybody did back in high school. He had that wonderful gift of friendship. Even the geeks liked him because Alan was kind to them when all the other popular kids ignored them. And he was so cute even with the acne that made him self-conscious and super shy with girls. But I drew him out, got him to talk. I was good at that.

It's amazing how well I remember our beginning even though it was half a century ago. It's twenty-four years since we divorced—a lifetime, really. I'm long remarried and live in Manhattan with my husband. New friends—a new life certainly without all the stress and anxiety of living with Alan. Funny—Alan and I get along now. After all, we have a history and three children that will always bind us.

We went together through high school and off and on during college. The "offs" were mostly when I pushed for an exclusive relationship and Alan pushed back. In retrospect, that should have told me something about Alan and about me too. The truth is that I never thought about marrying anyone except Alan. And when we did get married in Los Angeles where my folks lived, I thought that we would live happily ever after. Remember, it was the 1950s, and that's how it was supposed to be.

We bought a new 1959 Renault Dauphine with wedding money we received. Our plan was to drive the Dauphine across the country to Chicago where we had grown up to start our married life. Chicago was Alan's idea, and reluctantly I agreed, but I wasn't sure that I really wanted to return there. I had spent the last two and a half years at UCLA, and I loved it in Los Angeles where the weather was mild and where I had loads of new friends and no old baggage. And, of course, my parents. Returning to Chicago, where I hadn't lived in almost three years, scared me. And I was pretty sure that Alan's parents weren't happy about our marriage, especially his mother, who I was sure suspected that I wanted to trick Alan into getting me pregnant way back in high school. Can you imagine! Heavy necking was about all the sex Alan and I ever had until we married. Certainly that was part of the problem—sex. You have to understand in the 1950s "good girls" didn't give up their virginity until they married Mr. Right. I'm not saying that I didn't have urges. I did, but waiting till you were safely married was a rule drilled into all of us girls by our parents, teachers and friends. All of us got the message, which also included the guarantee that once we were married, the sexual experience would be absolutely perfect. Of course, it wasn't. I know that Alan was disappointed. I was too, although I wouldn't admit it even to myself. Mostly, I blamed myself. Obviously I was doing something wrong—something unwomanly. Alan and I should have talked about our "problem," but we never could, and so that failure became a permanent part of our marriage.

It didn't help to reduce my anxiety that from the start Alan complained about the Dauphine. He never liked the car. He said that it was unreliable and insubstantial. That was the word he used, *insubstantial*. He said that the VW Beetle was a much better car for the money, but I thought that it looked weird, and I pointed out that it had only two doors compared to the Dauphine's four. So, our trip to Chicago got off to a bad start with me nervous about the move and Alan grumbling about the car. I'm pretty sure other things were also bothering him.

Like a self-fulfilling prophecy, the Dauphine broke down just west of Salt Lake City. I think that Alan was almost glad. He didn't say so, but I know that he wanted to say, "I told you so." When that warning light popped on, I was terrified. My God, we were in the middle of the desert. It was blistering hot, and we were in this desolate place—just sand and rocks and probably snakes. I was sure that the car would blow up anytime. The terrifying warning light stayed on all the way to Salt Lake City. By that time, I hated Alan.

I'm not sure how we found the car repair shop, but we wound up at this place that looked like an army camp—Quonset huts and everything ultraclean—not like any auto repair shop I'd ever seen. And the mechanic we talked to looked like a doctor with his starched shirt and clipboard. All the mechanics looked like that. They were like a cult. The place freaked me out. The mechanic we talked to—I think his name was Frank—told us he didn't know anything about French cars, but that didn't make any difference to Alan. He just told this Frank guy to see what was wrong with the Dauphine. It didn't make any sense to me, but Alan just ignored me and gave Frank the go-ahead.

We had to wait in what Frank called the customer lounge, which was nothing more than a stuffy little room crowded with a bunch of strange types—all of them seemed to be fascinated by the black-and-white TV playing old episodes of *Gunsmoke*. I never liked Westerns, and I especially hated *Gunsmoke*. It seemed like hours until creepy Frank came to tell us that it would take them two days to fix the car and that it would cost something like $500. When I heard that, I exploded. Can you imagine spending two days in this godforsaken place? And I told Alan so—this Frank crook too. You would have thought that Alan would have understood. Not a chance—he even sided with Frank. I started screaming. I'll admit it. I didn't care.

"What the hell is wrong with you, Alan? I'm not going to be stuck in this awful place for two days. And where do you think we'll get the money to pay these thieves?"

That jerk Frank didn't like that and told me to calm down. Alan didn't even defend me. Instead, he actually agreed with Frank and told me to take it easy—that we could have a grand old time exploring wonderful Salt Lake City. Why didn't Alan understand? I was in this foreign place in the middle of nowhere. We didn't know a soul. We were running out of money. I was surrounded by weird people. Look,

I was afraid I needed support. I felt alone, and I desperately needed a friend. And my husband was against me. Can you blame me? I started to cry and yell.

"You're an idiot, Alan. I am not hanging around here for two days—and I bet it'll be more. If you want to stay here, fine, but I'm not."

Alan told me that I was crazy—that we didn't have any choice. But we did, and I said so.

"You stay. I'll go."

"Go how?"

"I'll fly to Chicago. You can wait here till the car is fixed and then drive to Chicago."

"That's the stupidest thing that I ever hear. What the hell is wrong with you? It's just two goddamn days."

"I don't care what you think. I'm out of here."

And that's what I did. I took a taxi to the Salt Lake City airport and flew to Chicago. Remember, I was twenty-one years old, and I was scared and angry. In retrospect, going over it fifty years later, maybe I was wrong to leave my new husband and run away. I know that, but I know something else now: Alan and I were a very bad fit. If I had known myself better back then, I would have realized that Alan and I never should have married. I think that I thought a lot about that all the way back to Chicago. But divorce, especially so fast, was something that I just couldn't consider. Almost no one got divorced in 1959. How could I face my family and friends? So, when Alan phoned me at my brother's apartment in Chicago and said that he was sorry and would be in Chicago the following day, I was actually relieved. I told him that I was sorry too. Maybe things would be better now.

We struggled through twenty-five years of a lousy marriage. I wish that I had had the maturity and courage to have seen then what is now so obvious. Salt Lake City was a warning—and a chance to get out of a bad situation and to make a new start—but I didn't understand. I'm pretty sure that Alan didn't either.

Zady

The joke was that my grandfather Jacob Lubin was a horseman. The word was meant to convey a person of substance who owned, bred, or at the very least rode horses. Years later when I actually knew people who were horsemen and horsewomen, I'd kid them that my grandfather had been a horseman. My intention was not to deceive or to pretend that my forebearers were wealthy elitists. They knew that I came from a modest middle-class background. So the gag was intentionally on me. In truth, Jake had been around horses most of his life. He and my uncle Benny had immigrated to the United States from around the Ukranian city of Kiev in the early twentieth century. Jake had married Benny's sister, Sarah. The brothers-in-law owned a junk wagon, a wobbly wooden cart pulled through the narrow alleys of Chicago in the 1940s and '50s by an old mare called Cookie.

"Rags, scrap, knives sharpened," they shouted as they followed their routes on the West Side of the city every weekday.

Jake lived with my parents, my brother and me on the north side in Rogers Park. My grandmother lived with us too, until she died in 1947. When my grandfather got home from work, he smelled of horse, so he would take a very hot shower and scrub himself with Lava soap until his skin had a rosy, healthy glow, the sour house smell replaced by a sharp medicinal scent.

Jake always returned to our apartment at about three in the afternoon. I could expect to see him when I came home from elementary school. He would always ask me the same question in his peculiar English.

"How are your studies doing, Joseph?"

Inevitably, I'd answer, "Fine, Zady."

"You gotta study hard, Joseph, if you don't want to be a schlepper."

"I know, Zady."

We didn't say much more, but I think that I took it for granted that Zady would be there every school day. Then one cold Tuesday in late March, he wasn't.

I asked my mother, "Where's Zady, Ma?"

"I don't know. He's usually home by now. Maybe he's helping Benny with something."

"But he's always here."

"Don't worry. I'm sure he'll be home soon."

I wasn't exactly worried. Maybe it was just that seeing Jake when I came home from school was part of the routine that I expected.

When Jake hadn't come home by five o'clock, I knew that my mother was concerned. The nickel that she dropped into our phone box made a clink when she dialed my aunt Bertha, Uncle Benny's wife. But Bertha didn't know where Benny was, and from what I heard of my mother's side of the conversation, Bertha was anxious.

It was dark now, and when my dad got home from work at around six, he and my mom spoke in hushed tones.

"Look, Lill, if anything was wrong, we'd hear something. Maybe the wagon broke down."

"Why didn't he call?"

"You know your father—he doesn't like to use the phone. I'm not even sure he knows how."

"He knows how if he has to."

The loud ringing of the phone interrupted the conversation. My mother quickly answered. I could see by the look on her face as she listened to the caller that this was not good news. When my mother spoke, it was with a sense of urgency.

"Yes, I know where it is. We'll be there right away."

"What is it, Lill?" my dad asked.

"It's Edgewater Hospital. My dad's had a heart attack. He's there with Benny." She took a deep breath and grabbed my father's hand.

"The nurse said to get there as fast as we can. Oh my God, Phil. I think it's bad—really bad."

"Don't get ahead of yourself. He's going to be okay. The car's downstairs. We'll be there in fifteen minutes."

"What about the kids?"

"I'll get the Lipmans. I'm sure they can watch them for us."

The Lipmans were our downstairs neighbors. We lived

on the second floor of a three-flat apartment building. The Lipmans occupied the first floor. I'd often play with Billy Lipman, who was my age, and our families were friendly. My folks dropped my brother and me off at the Lipmans'. Ida Lipman hugged my mother and said, "Lilly, it's going to be all right. Don't worry—we'll take care of the kids. Give us a call when you have a chance."

Then my mother turned to my brother, who was six years old, and to me, three years older, and told us:

"Behave yourselves, boys. Don't make any trouble for the Lipmans."

"When will you be back?" I asked.

"As soon as we can."

"Is Zady okay?"

"Don't worry, Joey," my father said. Zady's a tough guy. He'll be fine. Now, you boys be good, and we'll be back as soon as we can."

Then they were gone, and my brother and I stared confusedly at Mr. and Mrs. Lipman, wondering what was happening.

"I bet you guys haven't had dinner," Mr. Lipman said. "Ida, let's set a couple places at the table for Joey and Bobby."

It felt strange eating dinner at the Lipmans'. Although I often had snacks and sometimes lunch at the Lipmans', never before had I stayed for dinner. Now my brother and I sat at the maple dining room table, which had been expanded by the addition of a leaf to accommodate Bobby and me, Mr. and Mrs. Lipman, as well as Billy and his twelve-year-old sister, Sandra, who always ignored me. I liked the Lipmans, but I didn't feel that I belonged there, and I hoped that my mom and dad would soon come back and that Zady would be okay.

The next thing that I remember, my dad was waking me and Bobby. It took me a moment to realize that I was on the sofa in the Lipmans' apartment and not in my own bed.

"Come on, boys," my dad said. "You need to get up."

"Where are we going?" I mumbled.

"Up to our place."

"What time is it?"

"It's two o'clock."

"Where's Ma?"

"She's at the hospital."

"Why isn't she here?"

"She's taking care of things there."

"Where's Zady?"

"He's with your mom at the hospital. Come on now. I'm gonna take you and Bobby upstairs. You need to get some sleep."

"When will mom and Zady be home, Dad?"

"Let's get you guys upstairs and to bed, and we'll talk about everything in the morning."

———◦《◉》◦———

Bobby and I were tired, but we couldn't sleep.

"How come Ma and Zady aren't home from the hospital?" Bobby asked me.

"I don't know."

"Is he okay?"

"I don't know."

"What's wrong with Zady?"

"I'm not sure."

"Is it bad?"

"Bad enough for him to be in the hospital."

"What's a heart attack?"

"Where did you hear that?"

"I heard Ma tell Dad."

"It's not a good thing."

"Is Zady going to die?"

"No, didn't you hear dad say that Zady is a strong guy?"

"But a heart attack sounds very bad."

"Go to sleep, Bobby. We gotta go to school tomorrow."

"I don't know if I can sleep."

"Try."

———◆———

We did eventually fall asleep, and when we awoke in the morning, my dad told us that we didn't have to go to school.

"How come?" I asked.

"Boys, brush your teeth and wash up, and then your mother and I will talk to you."

"Where's Zady?" Bobby and I asked at the same time.

"We'll talk about it after you wash up."

Then my mother came into our bedroom. She looked very tired. Her eyes were red and swollen, but her hair was carefully combed, and her voice was clear.

"Phil, we should talk to them now. Joey, Bobby—your

Zady died last night at the hospital." Then her voice broke, and she started to softly sob.

"You know he loved you boys very much," she said.

Bobby and I didn't know what to say or do. The concept of death was new to us. We had never personally known anyone who had died. My grandma Sarah had died when I was an infant and before Bobby was born. Death was something remote—something that happened to other people, not to our Zady. And we had never seen my mother cry.

"But Zady wasn't even sick," I blurted.

"Zady had a heart attack," my father said.

"I don't know what that is."

"It means there was something wrong with his heart. It wasn't working right."

I wanted to ask more questions, but it seemed wrong to ask them now, so I just said that I was sorry, and Bobby said so too.

My parents decided that Bobby and I would not attend Zady's funeral. I think that they felt that we were too young, that the experience might be traumatic for us. I didn't say anything, but I was afraid about being at the funeral. I had heard that the dead person's body was displayed, and I didn't want to see Zady's that way. So the funeral was out for my brother and me, but we were allowed to be present for shiva, which was conducted at our apartment. Although sitting shiva is supposed to be a somber occasion, my recollection is of kind of a weeklong party with delicious food from Friedman's Deli: lox, herring, thick piles of sliced turkey, salami, corned beef, tongue and cream cheese, bagels, rye bread, rugelach and strudel. Everyone seemed to eat heartily, and there was as much laughter as tears. Later in life, I equated sitting shiva to an Irish wake without the deli and lasting longer.

All my aunts and uncles paid their respects. I knew all of them. Aunt Bessie with the mustache who always pinched my cheek so hard it hurt, Aunt Gladys who smelled of lilacs and Aunt Thelma whom my parents said was a Communist. There was Uncle Charles, who gave Bobby and me quarters every time he saw us, and Uncle Harold, who had divorced his first wife and married a young shiksa. There were also some friends of Zady who came, but I didn't know any of them. They were from his junk business and they chain-smoked and talked in rapid Yiddish.

———◦《◦》◦———

Near the end of the week, Uncle Benny took me aside. Benny was built like a barrel. Although he was a quiet gentle man, his strength was legendary. It was said that Benny could carry a cast-iron potbelly stove under each of his arms.

"How are you doing with this, Joey?"

"I don't know. It's just strange. Like, Zady was just here and, you know, alive, and now he isn't. I'm not used to him not being here. Uncle Benny, do you thing I'll get used to it?"

"Joey, after a while, we'll all get used to it. That's life, boychik. We live, and we die. In between, we try to have a good life."

"Did Zady have a good life?"

"I think that there was a lot of good in it. You and Bobby—that was part of the good for sure."

"Sometimes I wasn't so good. Sometimes Bobby and I made a lot of noise when Zady wanted us to be quiet, but he almost never yelled at us."

"Zady loved you boys, believe me."

"I wish I had talked to him more. I didn't talk to him that much."

"What you need to remember is that your Zady loved you and that he was a mensch. Do you know what a mensch is, Joey?"

"Not exactly."

"It's a good man. Someone who always tries to do the right thing even when that's very hard. I knew your Zady for forty years—good times and bad. He was a fair man. Never cheated anybody. Everyone knew that about him. Your Zady was a mensch. When you think of him, try to remember that."

Now I'm older than Zady was when he died. I think about him and about my own mortality, and I hope that when I'm no longer here, my grandchildren will be able to say that I was a mensch.

Going Home

The Lakewood Homes proffers neither a lake nor a wood. The assisted living facility does, however, attempt to provide a suitable substitute for the residents' previous homes. An attractive one-story building, Lakewood Homes is set on two-and-a-half acres of well-tended grounds in the northwest Chicago suburb of Barrington. There are eighty single-bedroom apartments, each approximately four hundred square feet and all with private bathrooms. Residents enjoy wide, well-carpeted hallways, a spacious dining area and almost as large a recreation room. And while there is no lake nor wood, there is a small pond bordered, that time of year, by beds of white and red roses.

Almost every one of the eighty apartments is occupied by an elderly man or woman, rarely both. These residents all suffer from Alzheimer's disease or from some form of dementia. Physical impairment ranges from minor to being unable to dress or feed themselves. Care at Lakewood is generally efficient and mostly compassionate. Monthly charges average over $5,000 for each resident.

Sid Cashman, a Lakewood resident, has been diagnosed

with Alzheimer's, which has not progressed to a point where he does not recognize his old friend Dan Berger. Not yet.

One image of Lakewood Homes dominates Dan's mind. It occurred on his first visit to the recreation room. About twenty residents stare at the large television screen. Perhaps half seem to be aware of what is playing on the TV. The others sleep fitfully or talk aggressively to themselves or to no one who is actually present. Two souls have obviously soiled themselves. One poor woman pulls violently on her hair. Try as he may, Dan cannot erase these disturbing pictures from his mind. The fact that this scene does not much change on Dan's subsequent visits to Lakewood does not help to diminish the memory.

Dan makes the drive to Lakewood from his home in Chicago's Lincoln Park neighborhood once a month—about fifty miles round trip. Dan doesn't exactly dread these visits, but he does not especially look forward to them. On one hand, Sid appears pleased to see him, and this in itself makes the long trip worthwhile.

The problem for Dan is that the visits leave him depressed. Dan and Sid are about the same age—eighty-two. Dan cannot avoid the chilling thought of himself someday in the not distant future living out of his life in a place like Lakewood. This affliction, or something like it, happened to Sid—why not Dan?

The two men met as freshmen at the University of Michigan in Ann Arbor. They became close during their undergraduate years and then throughout law school at the University of Chicago. Sid had a long and distinguished career with the Illinois State Attorney's Office, culminating as a well-respected superior court judge. Dan built one of the area's most successful tax practices. The Berger and Cashman families are close—wives, children and now grandchildren. The families worship at the same synagogue and often join each other on vacations. Two years ago, at a Cubs game, Sid told Dan that he had received a diagnosis of Alzheimer's. It was not a complete surprise. Dan and his wife, Vicky, had suspected something amiss in Sid for about a year, and Sid's wife, Carol, had expressed her concern about her husband's mental state to Vicky before Sid brought it up at the baseball game. One night at dinner at Gibson's on Rush Street, Sid was unable to figure the correct tip to leave the server. Dan made a benign joke of it, but afterward when the parking attendant brought their Lexus, Dan asked Vicky to drive home because he was so upset about Sid's confusion.

Now Dan visits his old friend once a month. Sometimes with Vicky. Conversation is becoming more difficult, although the subjects discussed rarely change: old times and old pals, Sid's activities that day, the quality of food (bland) and housekeeping (good) at Lakewood, their respective families and the Cubs. Sid struggles with memory and concentration. He frequently cannot remember what they had talked about. So, Sid raises the same questions again and again. The old friends used to exchange corny jokes. Now when Dan comes to a punch line, Sid stares uncomprehendingly at him. Dan is exhausted even before the long drive back to Chicago.

Carol Cashman savors her glass of prosecco as she curls up on the Bergers' sofa. For the first time in weeks, she is relaxed. Carol looks forward to these dinners with Dan and Vicky Berger. It gives her a chance to get away from the constant stress of coping with the anxiety that increasingly occupies her life. Dan and Vicky are her closest friends. She trusts them—feels safe in sharing her doubts and worries.

"I can't tell you how good this feels. So calm. It's been a long time. I'm enjoying myself. Thanks for dinner. Thanks for being such good friends."

"I wish that Sid could be here," Dan says.

"I do too, but I don't think that's in the cards," Carol replies.

"What do you mean?" Vicky asks.

"Let's be honest. Sid's not coming home. He's not getting better. I'm not going to pretend otherwise."

"I thought he was a little sharper when we saw him last week," Vicky hopefully suggests.

"Vicky, we all love Sid, but this disease is cruel. The doctors say that his mind will progressively decline. I—all of us—need to accept that reality."

"I guess you're right, Carol, but I just don't want to believe it," Dan sighs.

"Dan, I fight this every day. I lie to myself—maybe somehow he'll get better, a new drug, something. But it's all just false hope. I've got to deal with what is—not with what I hope. The Sid we all love is fading away more every day."

"How long can it go on like this?" Vicky asks.

"Years. Bob Golden has been in one of these places like Lakewood for seven years. He doesn't recognize his wife, Liz, anymore. He barely speaks. She told me that they're running out of money."

"My God!" Dan says shaking his head in disbelief.

"My dear friends," Carol replies, choosing her words carefully, "Sid is not a rich man. A judge doesn't make a lot of money. Our resources will run out long before seven years."

"Carol. I know that Lakewood is expensive, but I didn't realize how tight money is. Do you have a plan? Can your kids help? Maybe we can all pitch in," Dan offers.

"You're a prince, Dan, but frankly, I don't have a plan just yet. I don't know what I'm going to do."

———— ((●)) ————

Sid Cashman likewise has no plan. Long-term thinking tires and frightens him. It's better for him to take things minute by minute. As he does every night, he gets into bed for what he hopes will be a couple hours of sleep. He starts to say his personal prayer that he has recited to himself for many years.

"Lord, thank you for the day and night and bless all my loved ones."

There is more, but for some time now he has been unable to finish his prayer. Sid gets lost as he struggles to remember the words. Some nights he can recall almost all the prayer but not tonight.

It's not terrible here at this place where he lives. What is it called? How long has he been here? He isn't sure. He surveys his small apartment: a narrow bed, chest of drawers, a couple of lamps, a TV placed on a metal stand; a bedside tabletop prominently displays a silver-framed photograph of a smiling family. His?

He has made some friends here. Sometimes they go on day trips that are interesting—to a museum or to a concert. Then in the dark of his room, more words of his prayer rotely come back to him.

"Thank you for Carol, and help me to conduct myself in such a manner that I merit your love, support and understanding. Forgive me for my sins and . . ." But then he can remember no more, and now he is sleepy.

———

Twenty-five miles south, Vicky and Dan watch the news in their Lincoln Park home, but their attention is elsewhere.

"How about insurance?" Vicky asks.

"I asked Carol. They don't have that kind of insurance. It's too expensive. Anyway, they don't have it."

"What do you think is going to happen?"

"I don't know, Vic. I'm not sure what the options are when their money runs out."

"That's awful."

"It might be a good idea to get everyone together—us, Carol, their kids. Explore the best options. Should we be doing that? Are we sticking our noses in their business? I just don't know if it's our right to do that."

"They're our dear friends. We just want to help."

"I hope they see it that way."

"I think we have to try."

"We should talk to Carol. See what she thinks. You know, Vicky, this whole thing with Sid really gets to me. A decent man lives a good life—productive, honest, does all the right things and winds up with nothing but lousy choices at the end. Something's wrong—not fair."

"I'll call Carol. We'll get together to talk."

"Yeah—sooner the better."

———◦《◦》◦———

Carol Cashman sets up her own meeting with her two children. Larry, like his father, is a is a lawyer. But he does not practice law. He is a professor at Loyola Law School in Chicago. His specialty is environmental law. Larry is fifty-two years old and has been married to Ellen for twenty-four years. They have two children—Leah and Ned, both college students. Sid and Carol's other child, Sarah, was married for sixteen years before her divorce two years ago. Sarah has a child, Oscar, a high school student. Sarah has returned to school and is pursuing a master's degree in psychology. Her plan, after earning her degree in about a year, is to work as a psychiatric social worker. Since the divorce, her parents have paid much of her expenses. Carol has told Larry and Sarah the purpose of this meeting, which takes place at the Cashman condominium on Lakeshore Drive near North Avenue.

"What does Dad remember, Mom?" Larry asks.

"He's pretty good at pretending that he remembers

everything. But then he'll forget your kids' names ... or yours and Sarah's—or even mine."

"What kind of medical help is he getting?" Sarah inquires anxiously.

"I know that the people at Lakewood treat your dad well. They're nice to him, but, look, he has Alzheimer's. There's no cure. He's not likely to improve no matter what they do. We have to accept that his mind is slipping away a little more every day. In a lot of ways, it's worse than cancer where you kind of know the odds. With Alzheimer's, the odds are all against you—only the timing is unknown. I can't imagine anything worse."

"What can we do, Mom?" Larry asks.

"That's why I want to talk to you. Frankly, right now, your dad is probably in the best place he could be. But" — Carol hesitated before continuing—"I don't know how long I can do this. It's very expensive. The money—at this rate will run out in less than two years, at the most."

"Then what?" Larry and Sarah asked almost simultaneously.

"Then we'll have to try to find a place that will cost less to provide his care."

"What about his judge's pension?"

"Kids—the end line is this. If your dad lives long enough—even if he doesn't know us or even himself—his care will leave me very little."

Both children looked at their mother with a combination of incredulity, despair and profound sadness.

"Maybe I can contribute something," Larry offers.

"I can find a job," Sarah adds.

"I appreciate the offer from both of you, believe me, I do,

but you have your own families to raise, your own lives, and I know that your budgets are tight. We're not out of money for now. I just want you to appreciate what's going on. What I need from you most is your understanding—your love."

"Love you can count on, Mom," Sarah quickly interjects.

"Love for sure, Mom. I only wish that I had a ton of money," Larry says.

Sid Cashman isn't thinking about money or about love. He's wondering where he put his car keys because he wants to drive into Chicago to visit his legal colleagues. He forgets that he does not have a car or that he no longer knows how to drive. And he cannot recall the names of his old associates or the location of the court in which he and they presided. The forgetting troubles him—a nagging feeling, an annoyance; then the feeling disappears. He is vaguely aware of Carol and that she visits. Often he wants to go home with her, but she tells him that he needs to stay at this place at least for a while longer. Lately, though, he thinks that he really would like to go home. The thing is maybe it's better for him here, and he's not sure how it will be if he returns home. His friend Lenny has been here longer than Sid, and he and Sid talk about things. Perhaps Lenny has some advice about Sid going home. Sid makes a point of discussing this later with Lenny and then forgets.

Summer moves into autumn, and Dan cannot deny the painful truth. Sid's condition is declining at a precipitous pace. When Dan comments to Sid about the vibrant color of the leaves on the oak tree outside the window of Sid's Lakewood apartment, his friend continues to stare at the painterly scene in silence.

"You're lucky you've got such a beautiful view, Sid."

No answer. Dan tries again.

"Remember when we used to drive all the way out to Highland Park on Sheridan Road in the fall to check out the wonderful colors of the leaves? How would you like to take a drive out there now?"

"Where?" Sid replies blankly.

"Highland Park."

"Is that far?"

"Not that far."

"How will we get there?"

"I'll drive."

"In your car?"

"Right."

"When?"

"Next time I come."

"Okay."

Sid continues to gaze blankly out the window. Dan says goodbye to his old friend, but Sid doesn't appear to notice when he leaves the room.

————)((O)) ————

A cruel winter storms into the Midwest, shrouding Lakewood Homes in a mantle of snow and ice. The wind chill factor is ten below zero. Sid Cashman hardly notices. Except the snow reminds him of the holidays. So now may be a good time for him to go home for the holidays and all the celebrations. But this woman doesn't agree. Her reluctance makes him angry. He screamed at her when she visited with those other people. Why doesn't she understand that it's time for him to leave this place? He's sorry that he lost his temper. He'll do much better at home, although he doesn't exactly remember where home is. It's a dim concept more than a tangible place. So ephemeral that he can't get his arms around it. And thinking about going home confuses him.

Is this why he's angry so often? His friend Lenny tells him that Sid's wife (he forgot her name) doesn't want him to come home—that she doesn't want him around to bother her. That can't be right. It's all frustrating and makes him anxious, though those words are no longer in his vocabulary, but the feelings are. He looks out his window at the snow and recalls skiing with Carol (that's the woman's name) and with those other people who visit him sometimes. Then, again, he thinks about going home.

————)((O)) ————

"So, the gang is all here," Dan announces.

And indeed, they are all in attendance at the Bergers' Lincoln Park home: Dan and Vicky Berger, Carol Cashman and her two children—Larry and Sarah. They are all seated around the spacious, glass dining-room table. Two large pepperoni-and-mushroom pizzas along with a garbanzo salad are on the table. The purpose of the ordered-in dinner is to discuss the present and future of Sidney Joseph Cashman, resident now for sixteen months of Lakewood Homes, Barrington, Illinois.

"I'm so glad that we're all together," Carol says. "It's a tough time, and it helps to talk to all of you."

"We love Sid, Carol. I think that the question is what's best for him," Dan says.

All present voice their agreement.

"The problem is it's not so easy to know what's best," Larry says. "I admit that I'm not sure. Are you, Mom?"

"Sometimes I think I am, and then I'm not at all certain," Carol replies.

"Well, I sure don't know what's right," Sarah says.

"Is there a right answer?" Vicky asks.

"What are the options? I mean, for now, it seems to me that the choices are: he stays at Lakewood. Or he comes home. What else is there?" Dan asks.

"For right now, you're right, Dan," Carol answers. "But when the money runs out in about a year, we'll have to find another place, if we can, that will take care of Sid for less money."

"Understood—we're talking about a one-year solution," Dan acknowledges.

"And what if he comes home?" Larry asks.

"I hope you all understand that I love my husband, but having him move back home with me isn't going to work. For one thing, I'd need a full-time nurse to help me, and that's very expensive."

"A full-time nurse?" Larry asks.

"Son, I'm almost eighty-two. I have trouble taking care of myself. It's hard to say this, but your dad is like a big baby. He can't really dress himself anymore or go to the toilet himself. Don't ask about eating. Even with full-time help, it's a terrible job."

"I didn't know that it had gotten that bad," Vicky says.

"Look, the truth is that the option of Sid coming home to live with me is not acceptable. I just can't do it."

"Carol," Dan says, "none of us is judging you or blaming you. It's an awful situation. We know that. We understand that you're doing the best you possibly can. I'm just so sorry—for you, for all of us, especially for Sid."

The conversation goes on for a while longer, but there really isn't much more to talk about. Sid has been dealt a very bad hand and is destined to play it out at Lakewood Homes. Everyone seated around the dining-room table loves Sid. And each one in his or her heart knows that love is not nearly enough.

Sid lies awake fully dressed in his bed at Lakewood Homes. It's dark. Ordinarily, he would be sleeping, but tonight his head is flooded with thoughts, which flicker so quickly that it is impossible for him to retain any of these impressions for more than a second or two: the bright color of autumn leaves, the laughter of a young woman, a man in a judge's robe, the smooth glide down a ski slope. He switches on a lamp. He studies the faces in the silver-framed photograph atop the bedside table. Who are these people? For an instant, he almost remembers; then, like smoke, recognition vanishes. It's hot in his room, and he sweats. He opens his ground-floor window a little and gulps in the cold, early-spring air. Better. He raises the window and stumbles outside onto the sparse lawn. He can just make out the shapes of the still-barren trees. His steps are the only sound in the night. He moves slowly, uncertainly toward the trees until he comes to the pond. He hesitates for a moment before wading into the frigid black water. His teeth chatter. His legs numb, but he moves farther into the water. Suddenly he remembers those faces in the photograph. How good to remember. Then he plunges deeper. He's going home.

Quiet Studio Apartment

STUDIO APARTMENT
One block from shopping center, next to park.
Clean, quiet. Gas, water, parking included.
$585/month.
Call Mr. Harvey at 312 111 1111

In the seven years that I had owned the fifteen-unit apartment building located in Elgin, a suburb northwest of Chicago, things had always been mostly quiet. All of the apartments were studios best suited for occupancy by one person. The majority of the tenants were single men, most of whom worked in factories or warehouses or were retired. Only a few earned more than $35,000 a year. Occasionally, someone would party noisily, but mostly, as the classified ad in the local paper stated, it was quiet.

My favorite tenant was Walt Palmer. He was a retired carpenter who had lived in the building for twenty-three years. Walt always paid his rent right on time, and on those rare occasions when he needed something fixed like a leaky faucet, he was apologetic about bringing it to my attention.

Everybody liked Walt, which was understandable because he would often help other tenants when they needed a ride or a cigarette. And he was generous in other ways. As it turned out, too generous. He was an easy touch. Sometimes other tenants would borrow ten or twenty dollars from Walt. Sometimes he was paid back. Often not.

On Saturday mornings when I was at the building checking things out, I always made it a point to knock on Walt's door to make sure that he was okay. He was in his eighties, somewhat fragile, and his movements were stiff and a bit halting, but his mind was sharp. Every weekday morning at six, he went to a nearby fitness center for his workout.

On the last Saturday morning that I saw Walt, I asked him how he was feeling.

"Thanks for asking. Well, I'm a little creaky, and I'm getting so I can't hear a damn thing, but all in all, I can't complain."

His apartment, like all the others in the building, was one room with a kitchenette, a short hallway with closet and a bathroom, which included toilet, bathtub and shower. It was cluttered with the belongings acquired over a lifetime: a heavily scratched maple chest of drawers far too big for this space. A metal desk displayed framed black-and-white photographs of his long-dead wife and of his two children when they were young. A newer frame exhibited a color photograph of his granddaughter in her cheerleader outfit. The most prominent feature of the apartment was open cardboard boxes—about a dozen of them. Some contained unopened cans of soup, tuna or vegetables. Others held rolls of toilet paper. A few were filled with tools—wrenches, a hammer, a wire cutter, nails, and a large flashlight. The contents of other boxes were difficult to determine. Maybe old financial records. It was simply overflowing with stuff accumulated over the years. Far too much for this three-hundred-square-foot apartment.

I teased Walt that one day the stacked boxes were going to collapse on him.

"You're right—I keep meaning to get rid of a bunch of this junk. I'm not even sure what's in some of these boxes. I just don't seem to get around to it."

After my visit with Walt, I had to see another tenant, Ralph Clemens, in apartment seven, and I wasn't looking forward to it. I was threatening to evict Clemens, and I wanted to make sure that he would vacate his apartment by the following Saturday as he had promised. Ralph Clemens was a fifty-five-year-old electrician who could not seem to hold a job. I suspected that he had a problem with booze—maybe drugs too. Whatever his problems, he was two months behind on his rent. Clemens was a long-divorced father of three grown children, two of whom had nothing to do with him. He was always polite to me. He said the right things but did the wrong things. According to some of the other tenants, he kept company with some bad characters. The stench of stale beer and cigarettes filled the close space of his apartment.

"Ralph, I want to make sure that you'll be out by next Saturday."

"No problem, boss. I already got a lot of my stuff packed." He pointed to several boxes filled with clothing.

"How about the furniture?"

"I got a couple buddies to help me with that. And like I said, I'll leave the keys in the office before I go. Not to worry."

"I'm not worried, Ralph. I just want to make sure that we're on the same page. And that you don't leave me a mess when you're gone."

"No way. It'll be cleaner than when I moved in."

Ralph smiled broadly when he spoke, exposing a gap where one of his eyeteeth should have been.

"I wish I had the cash to stay, but like I told you, I haven't had any real work in a long time, and I'm tapped out. It's so bad that I have to move in with my daughter till I find something. Fifty-five and living with my kid. Christ!"

After my conversation with Ralph Clemens, I went to my office, which shared space in the building's small laundry. My janitor, Angel Gomez, greeted me when I opened the door.

"So, Señor Harvey, is numero seven out by Saturday?"

Angel Gomez had been my janitor since I bought the building. He was a Mexican who had come to the United States illegally forty years ago when he was twenty. An American citizen for twenty years, he lived with his wife and his youngest child in a house he owned about a mile from the apartment building. His other older three children were married and had their own families. Angel's main job was working at a can-manufacturing company in the area. He had been there for twelve years and earned eighteen dollars an hour. He was dependable, honest, could fix just about anything. And I trusted his judgment. Over seven years of working together, we had developed an easy working relationship. Angel had a dry, ironic sense of humor.

"He says I shouldn't worry. He'll be out Saturday."

"I think it's good he's gone. I hear he spends all his money on drugs and then asks other tenants for loans."

"Well, if he's not out by Saturday, I'll have to move ahead with eviction, and that takes a while. Better that he leaves on his own."

"I say fifty-fifty he moves out by Saturday."

"So, you don't believe him?"

"Without the drugs, maybe, I believe. But with the drugs, not so much."

"We'll see by Saturday."

I was home the following Thursday night about ten o'clock watching a Bulls game on television when I received a call from Walt Palmer's daughter, Sally. She told me that Walt had died earlier that day. She had called him as she usually did in the afternoon and again about dinnertime. Concerned that he hadn't returned her calls, which was not like her dad, she and her husband had gone to the apartment and found Walt dead in his bed.

"You know, Mr. Harvey, my dad was eight-six, but it's still a shock. I just didn't expect him to die—not now, anyway."

"I didn't either, Sally. Your dad seemed to be in pretty good shape. I'm so sorry. I liked him. Is there anything I can do, Sally?"

"No, we're okay. It'll just take us some time to get all the stuff out of the apartment. I'm sure you know, my dad was something of a packrat."

"Take as much time as you need."

————))((((((O)))))((————

The next Saturday, as usual, I was at the building. The three tenants I encountered commented sadly about Walt's passing—all noting what a nice man he was. Angel was stoic.

"It's life, my friend. Walt was very old. I think it was his time."

"I guess, but I'm sorry. Anyway, life goes on. Let's see about number seven. He's supposed to be out today."

"I checked. He no move."

"Damnit! I'm going to talk to him right now."

————))((((((O)))))((————

"What's going on, Ralph? You're supposed to be out today, and you're still here."

"Man, I've been sick all week. Look, I've got just about everything packed," Ralph said, gesturing at what appeared to be many stacked and taped cardboard boxes.

"Look, Ralph, you said you'd be out today. You're not. All your furniture is right where it was last week."

"I've made arrangements to move it all to my daughter's tomorrow and Monday. I would have done everything when I told you, but I was really sick. I've been throwing up—big-time flu."

And when I looked closer, he did look terrible. His skin

was sallow, his eyes bloodshot. He had difficulty standing still. His entire body shook. He clasped his hand together in a futile attempt to stop them from trembling. And he appeared to have some difficulty breathing.

"I tell you what, Ralph. I'll give you till Tuesday. If you're not out—completely out—by then, you're gonna get a notice to evict."

"I'll be gone by Monday at the latest. You can count on it." Then he paused for a moment as to change the subject and continued, his voice almost a whisper.

"I guess you heard about the old man, Walt."

"Yeah, I did. It's too bad. He was a good man."

"Yeah, he was. I'm really sorry."

I'm not sure that I believed Clemens would be out by Monday, but the truth was that, if I had to evict him, it would probably take two months and cost me plenty in legal costs. I suspected that Ralph Clemens knew that too.

Monday afternoon I phoned Angel to see if Clemens had moved out. Angel told me that, as of that morning, Ralph Clemens was still in the apartment. Son of a bitch, I thought. Now I'd have to evict him. Aggravation and lost rent were what I was contemplating. I called Clemens and received a message telling me that that number was not in service. I figured that I would wait until tomorrow and then serve Clemens with the five-day eviction notice. This is going to be an all-around pain in the ass.

My first reaction when I got the phone call from Detective Kevin Donaldson of the Elgin Police Department was that he was calling for a donation to the Police Officers Fund or something like that. But quickly I could tell by his grave tone that this was about something else.

"Mr. Harvey, are you the owner of the building at _____?"

"I am. Is there a problem?"

"There may be, and we need your help."

"What do you mean?"

"We're investigating the death of Walter Palmer."

"Yes, he just passed away."

"We're investigating his death as a possible homicide."

"What are you saying? Walt was eight-six. I was told that he just died in his sleep."

"What I can tell you confidentially is that some things have come to our attention that lead us to suspect that Mr. Palmer's death may not be from natural causes."

"Like what, murder?"

"Right now, we don't know, but there's an ongoing investigation. What I'd like you to do is to say nothing about this to any of the tenants or, for that matter, to anyone else."

"Of course, I won't say anything."

"I'll let you know what's going on, and we may need your cooperation down the road."

"Whatever you need. I can't imagine anyone harming Walt."

"That's what we're investigating. Thanks, Mr. Harvey. We'll be in touch."

I couldn't believe what I had just heard. Kindly old Walt Palmer murdered. That was the terrible word. In my building. What a frightening thought. Who? Why? This seemed impossible—the kind of thing that never involved people like me.

I didn't have to wait long for answers. The next afternoon, I received a phone call from Detective Donaldson. Ralph Clemens had been arrested for the murder of Walt Palmer and had quickly confessed to strangling Palmer. The motive was robbery. Clemens had gone to Walt's apartment to ask for a "loan." When the elderly man refused, Clemens choked him to death and laid Walt's body on his bed. He took all the cash in Walt's wallet—$107. Clemens was being held in the Elgin city jail.

"Are you there, Mr. Harvey?" Detective Donaldson asked.

"Yeah, I'm just so shocked, I don't know what to say. I don't get it."

"Clemens told us that he was in a drugged haze and didn't know what he was doing. He says he didn't mean to kill the old guy—that things got out of control."

"For $107. To murder a good man. It doesn't make sense."

"I wish I could tell you that we don't see this kind of crime, but we do. And you're right. It doesn't make sense."

The public defender appointed to represent Ralph Clemens was a young man named Mason Cruz. He spoke to his client in a businesslike manner. Clemens had confessed—had described in precise detail his murder of Walter Palmer. Unless he wished to retract his confession, the issue was not one of guilt or innocence; he was clearly guilty. The question for Clemens, Cruz said, was one of mitigating circumstances. Specifically, Clemens being under the influence of drugs when he committed the murder. This plea, if successful, would not shield Clemens from a long prison term, but it might offer him the possibility of freedom sometime in the distant future. In a way, he was fortunate that Illinois had recently banned the death penalty. At best, Cruz bluntly advised Clemens, he would spend at least the next twenty years in prison. Did it make a difference that he hadn't meant to kill the old man or that he didn't have a criminal record? he asked Cruz. Yes, those factors would be considered in his defense, but even so, Cruz advised, he was looking at many years behind bars.

<hr />

Alone in his cell, Ralph Clemens was surprised at how quiet it was. He had always heard that prisons were noisy—the slamming of heavy metal doors, the shouts of prisoners. He guessed that in a real prison it would be that way. The Elgin jail had only three cells, and his was the only one occupied. He hated the silence. It was like being buried in a tomb. What now? The rest of his life in prison. How had this happened? He didn't think of himself as an evil man. Killing the old man was terrible, but it was an accident. But he had killed him—murdered him. Murdered a nice old guy who never did anything to harm him—who had loaned him money many times. He had choked him till he was dead. That was reality. The fucking heroin was to blame. *Jesus Christ, what have I done?* Did it matter that he didn't mean to kill the old man? Not to the old man. Not to the old man's family. He, Ralph Clemens, had murdered the man they all loved. Who loved Ralph Clemens? Not his family. His daughter was the only one who had talked to him since his arrest, and she mostly cried during that brief conversation. His two sons—they had had nothing to say to him for years. Certainly that would not change now. The rest of his life in prison. That was what he was looking at. All the lost jobs, the drugs and booze, the bad women, the lies, the people he had let down, the bullshit that was his life. He never thought it would turn out like this. He was a murderer, and he was going to spend the rest of his lousy life buried in prison. He deserved it. No matter how he tried to get around it, he had choked the life out of Walt Palmer. It sickened him to admit what he had done. Now what? Twentysome years or more without freedom, being told what to do every hour every day. He couldn't do it. The truth was his life was over. *For a change, do something. Right. There's no place for you—anywhere.*

About three that morning in the almost total silence of his cell, Ralph Clemens carefully knotted two of his bed-sheets together and hanged himself from a ceiling light fix-ture. He did not break his neck but slowly strangled to death much as he had murdered Walt Palmer.

The following day I received a phone call from Detective Donaldson informing me of Ralph Clemens's suicide.

"This whole thing, Detective, is like a horror story. Two men dead for I don't really know why. I keep thinking that if I had evicted him earlier, all this might not have happened."

"You'll make yourself crazy thinking like that. What if this, what if that. Forget about it. Nobody could have predicted this. You know, Mr. Harvey, this guy kind of fooled us. He didn't seem like a potential suicide, or we would have had eyes on him. I'm not saying he wasn't down, you know, depressed, but he was always talking to anybody who would listen, saying he wasn't really a murderer—that everything had been a horrible mistake. Always talking. I didn't figure him for a suicide."

"How can you tell?"

"Sometimes you can't, and this guy was a great bullshitter."

Whereabouts Unknown

I spent about a half hour studying the black-and-white photograph that an old pledge brother had emailed me. The picture of my Phi Epsilon Pi fraternity pledge class (1958) showed sixteen young men each dressed in sports jacket and tie. Think Brooks Brothers. Short hair, no beards. The expression *clean-cut* comes to mind. All of us are smiling, brandishing orthodontically straightened white teeth as we look with optimism into the future. The year 1954 was that kind of time. The place was the University of Illinois at Urbana-Champaign. *Father Knows Best* was big on TV. Everyone was talking about Marlon Brando in *On the Waterfront*. Elvis was just getting started. Gas cost about twenty-five cents a gallon. A new house could be had for a little over $10,000. Grandfatherly President Dwight Eisenhower signed the new social security bill into law. Zealous Communist hunter Joe McCarthy was censored by his fellow senators. As I said, it was that kind of time.

Of the sixteen college freshmen in the photograph, three have died. The whereabouts of one, Barry Simon, are unknown. There's Barry in the front row. This story is about Barry.

I met Barry Simon at Senn High School on Chicago's North Side, although we were never what I would call friends. I suppose we didn't have that much in common, and as I think about it now over a half century later, that relationship didn't change when we both pledged Phi Ep. Barry struck me as a spoiled rich kid whose parents lived in a luxurious apartment on Lake Shore Drive. He was small in stature, more cute than handsome, and he had an annoying habit of giggling when he spoke. When I think of him, the word *soft* comes to mind. Barry had a terrific wardrobe, especially cashmere sweaters of which he possessed at least a dozen of various colors and styles. His stylish necktie collection was the envy of all of us pledges as well as house members: foulard, striped, solids, flowered—even bows. Occasionally, I would ask Barry if I could borrow one of these beauties. With great reluctance he would sometimes agree, but his conditions of quick return and his scrutiny of the returned tie for food stains or rough use were so rigorous that I stopped asking him, which was, of course, Barry's preference.

Barry was an average student enrolled in the school of commerce. But his interest in business was intense. Every day a copy of the *Wall Street Journal* was delivered to Mr. Barry T. Simon (*T* for Tyler). Barry T. read the *Journal* from cover to cover. Outside of schoolbooks, recreational reading for the rest of us involved purloined glimpses of the few copies of *Playboy* magazine that circulated throughout the fraternity house.

Why do I note that Barry and I had little in common? After all, we were both Jewish boys from the same high school. We knew many of the same people, attended some classes together. We had even once in a while dated the same girls. But the connection ended there. I was an athlete—a member of the Senn baseball and track teams. Barry's father owned several horses, one of which Barry rode on a private bridle path. My friends and I talked endlessly about the Chicago Cubs and Bears. Barry discussed at length on the vagaries of the stock market. My group learned about sex from prostitutes. Barry rarely talked about sex. We played serious poker and smoked cigarettes. Neither of these vices tempted Barry. I wouldn't say that Barry Simon was a bad guy. He just wasn't one of my guys.

Then all at once back in 1954, we were both pledges of the Phi Epsilon Pi fraternity. As I've noted, Barry and I didn't have the same interests. As a matter of fact, I think it would be accurate to say that none of my pledge brothers were tight with Barry. That did not, however, mean that we didn't get along. As pledge brothers, we had to, and that included the very disparate Barry Tyler Simon.

To understand Barry, a brief description of his parents is essential. His father, Lawrence J. Simon (I never learned what the *J* stood for) was also well-dressed. I didn't see him often, perhaps three or four times a year, but when I did, he was always clad in a well-tailored, three-piece, expensive suit, complemented by a starched white shirt and neatly arranged bow tie. His shoes were soft leather, polished to a high shine. He was a bit older than the other dads. Probably in his early sixties. Average in height and somewhat overweight. I got the impression that as a younger man he had been near handsome before he had gained pounds and lost most of his now-gray hair. Lawrence Simon projected success and authority, although, he wasn't loud or boastful. He was rich, and he was well-aware that everyone knew it.

When I think back these many years, I never saw Mr. Simon without his wife at his side. I don't know if the expression *trophy wife* was in vogue at that time, but I would say that characterization fit Jenny Simon quite well. She was, I'm guessing, in her early forties, almost as tall as Lawrence, and she was not averse to showing off her long, shapely legs. She favored tight-fitting sweaters that emphasized her impressive breasts. And she was pretty with a full, sensuous mouth and large hazel eyes. Long honey-blond hair completed the picture. Jenny Simon was hot and as far as any of us could imagine from the picture of our own mothers. I suppose that it's not surprising that every one of us pledges lusted for Jenny Simon, mother of Barry. Of course, none of us said a word to Barry about our lascivious thoughts. But how could he not know? To complicate Jenny matters, she kind of flaunted her sexuality when she was around us. Very strange, though, that this temptress—the image of our masturbatory desires—was the mother of our prissy pledge brother.

Mr. Lawrence Simon was a big real estate developer. His company acquired large tracts of rural property all over the United States and built homes on that property for the expanding suburban population. The rumor was that Lawrence Simon was already a rich man and was well on his way to amassing staggering wealth. Mr. Simon's only son, Barry, was the heir apparent to the Simon fortune. I was vaguely aware of this, but it didn't change my opinion of Barry. He was still sort of a jerk with an amazingly sexy mom.

It was in our sophomore year that I started to hear gossip

about the Simon business. There were hints of financial problems—lawsuits came to light. Then one day the *Wall Street Journal* (the newspaper that Barry read religiously) carried a feature article that stated that the Simon Company was accused by the government of bribing various local officials in order to receive favorable land acquisition deals. The story went on to say that the government meant to show that Lawrence Simon's criminal behavior would not be condoned. The government intended to make an example of Simon for any other lawbreaker. Lawrence J. Simon faced the possibility of up to ten years in prison.

As you might suspect, the effect on Barry of his father's alleged transgressions was profound. Given how closely his self-confidence was connected to his father's great wealth and power, how could it have been otherwise? The shame of Lawrence J. became the shame of Barry T. Had he turned to us pledge brothers for solace, he probably would have received our support, even our sympathy. But placing himself in that position of supplication was impossible for Barry. None of us was surprised when Barry withdrew from school. After a well-publicized trial ended in conviction, his father was sentenced to a prison term of three to five years. The Simon family proceeded to disintegrate. The luscious Jenny expeditiously filed for divorce. The marvelous Lake Shore Drive condo was sold to settle debt and fines—as were all other Simon assets that were searched for and discovered. The story faded; time passed. By my senior year, Lawrence Simon was released from prison. He tried to start another real estate development company, without success. The old magic and, of course, the old connections were missing. He earned a modest living selling mid-priced homes in one of the very suburbs that he had built years earlier.

Years later, I read his obituary in the *Chicago Tribune*, which noted that he had lived in the middle-class Logan Square neighborhood. He was seventy-one years old. His only survivor was listed as his only child, a son, Barry.

I'm not sure why I decided to attend the funeral. Maybe out of old respect for the once-great man I had known long ago. Maybe I was curious to see Barry, whom I had not heard from since our university days. So, I went to the Pizer Funeral Home on Skokie Boulevard in Wilmette—not sure what I expected. I had anticipated a standard funeral—one that embraced mourners and offered a rabbi to preside over the solemn occasion. Perhaps a number of speakers who would eulogize the deceased. Not so. This was a much smaller affair, which occupied a rather spare room about the size of a two-car garage. Clean, dimly lighted; a soft carpet muffled what sounds there were. Metal card chairs had been placed in two rows of seven, and at the front of the room, on a wooden easel, was a fine color photograph of Mr. Lawrence J. Simon obviously taken in his heyday. An unctuous attendant asked in a whisper if I wished to sign the visitation book. I did. There were only three other signatures on the lined page. Two of the signers were evidently already gone because the only other mourner in the room other than me was my old fraternity brother, Barry Simon.

Both of us were then in our early thirties. I was married, the father of two young children and was the creative director of a small, up-and-coming Chicago advertising agency.

My wife and I had recently bought our first home, a four-bedroom ranch style in Highland Park.

Given other circumstances, I probably would not have recognized Barry. It wasn't just that I hadn't seen him in a dozen years. The changes were more than physical. I introduced myself.

"Barry, it's David Markoff. My condolences. I was sorry to hear about your dad."

"Thanks for coming, Dave. I recognized you right away even though it's been a while since I've seen you."

"I know. Time kind of slips away."

Barry looked around the almost empty room and smiled—a sad smile.

"Not much of a turnout."

I didn't know what to say, and Barry quickly filled the void.

"People forget or maybe don't care. There was a time when hundreds would have shown their respects. But that was then, and now is a different story."

"I always liked your dad. Had he been ill?"

"He had a bad heart. Toward the end he was a very tired man. Not the big shot of the old days."

"I'm sorry to hear that, Barry."

"Anyway, I really appreciate that you're here. Catch me up on what's been going on in your life."

I told him about my wife and kids, about the new house and about my job. Barry seemed especially interested in my work.

"The ad business has always fascinated me."

"Well, it has its pluses and minuses. How about you, Barry, what have you been doing?"

"For a while after I left school, I sold life insurance—a real tough racket. Then after my dad got out of prison, the two of us started a company to build and market houses. But we just couldn't seem to make a go of it. And we didn't always see things the same way. Anyway, we closed that business. Dad got a job selling houses, and I landed a gig selling printing for Ira Richman. You may remember that Ira's family owned a big printing company. The job was okay, but it was hard to get ahead in that company with all the family members involved in the business. The last couple of years, I've kind of jumped from one thing to another: worked for an executive search firm, did some telemarketing, sold artificial flowers." Barry paused for a moment as though he was hoping for some kind of understanding. "I couldn't seem to catch a break."

"Maybe you just haven't yet found yourself. You're still a relatively young man, Barry."

"I'm thirty-three, Dave."

"That's not that old. You've got most of your life ahead of you."

As we talked, I had been looking closely at my old pledge brother. I said earlier that the change I had observed in him was more than physical. Yes, Barry was balding. He sported a potbelly and wore clothes somewhat out of style. The difference I realized was in attitude. Barry's old school days confidence—one might say overconfidence—had been replaced by a very large chip on his shoulder.

"Where are you living?" I asked Barry.

"I've got an apartment in a four-flat in my old neighborhood on Aldine just a block west of the Drive. I manage the building, so I get a good deal on the rent."

"How about your mom?

"She married a guy in the movie business. They live in Los Angeles. They're part of a show-biz crowd. We stay in touch, but you know how it is. She's got her own life, and I have mine. It's been over a year since I saw her."

"Look, Barry, let's get together—catch up. It's been too long."

The words just popped out of my mouth. I wasn't even sure that I wanted to see Barry. Could be I was sorry for him. He certainly didn't seem to have much going for him. Anyway, I asked him to meet.

"Sure, Dave, great." Barry pumped my hand with both of his.

We exchanged phone numbers, and I said that I would call him to set up a lunch. Then I made my way out of the visitation room at the Pizer Funeral Home. During the time that I was there, I noticed that no one else had paid their last respects to Mr. Lawrence J. Simon, who had once been a man of power and influence in Chicago.

——————————

Barry and I arranged to meet at the restaurant in the Wrigley Building on Michigan Avenue. It was convenient for me, as my office was in the building. Barry was right on time. He wore a well-pressed suit a bit out-of-date. His stripped tie, however, was au courant. After we were seated, I asked Barry if he wanted a drink.

"Thanks, Dave, but I'll pass. I'm trying to lay off the booze."

"You know, Barry, you're kind of a mystery man. You sort of disappeared. Do you see any of the old bunch?"

"No I really haven't. I went underground after I dropped out of school and"—here, Barry seemed to search carefully for the right words—"everything came out about my dad and the trial and all that. I kind of went into hiding. I didn't want to see anyone—didn't want to answer questions. You know, people can be real assholes."

The waiter came by to take our order. I ordered a steak sandwich, rare, and a draft beer. Barry addressed the waiter as though he were hard of hearing, speaking slowly like someone explaining a complicated problem.

"What I want is the small filet mignon, but I want it well-done on the outside—even a touch burned. Inside, and this is important, I require it pink— not red, pink. If the kitchen can't cook it exactly that way, I'll send it back. Understand?"

"Yes, sir," the waiter replied with professional courtesy. "Well-done on the outside and pink inside. I'm sure our kitchen will cook it to your satisfaction."

Barry then turned to me with the waiter still at tableside. "I just hope he doesn't screw it up."

"I'm sure he's got it straight," I said, wanting to change the subject from the instructions regarding the precise preparation of Barry's steak. I asked him, "By the way Barry. Are you solo? Not married? No significant other?"

"I had kind of a girlfriend. She worked at the artificial flower business where I worked. Let's just say she satisfied my physical needs. It was okay for a while, but it was never serious."

"What are you doing now—workwise?"

"Not a thing. Other than managing the apartment building, I'm looking for a full-time job. Maybe you could give me some advice. I've always been interested in advertising. Do you think I could get into it?"

I had seen this coming, but I wasn't sure what to tell Barry. What do you tell a guy in his thirties with absolutely no experience in advertising about landing a job in the business? Of more concern to me was that I didn't have any idea what skills Barry had. Was he a hard worker? Did he work well with others? I didn't even know if he was smart or, for that matter, honest or reliable. It had been a dozen years since I had seen him, and I couldn't say that I knew him well even back then. Sure, I wanted to give an old friend (was he actually a friend?) a hand when he was down on his luck. But I was kind of flying blind here.

"It's a tough business to break into. People think that advertising is a real glamorous business—exciting and creative, plenty of action, plenty of money, loads of entertaining and good times. There's some of that, but there's also a lot of pressure, long hours. Clients who can be real jerks."

"Sounds like some other jobs I've had."

"I bet."

"Do you think I could find a job in advertising?"

"To be honest with you, Barry, I don't know. I think you're a bright guy. You might do great. I can't say. I'm not even sure what part of the business would be best for you. I suppose account management would be the likeliest place for you—to start, anyway."

"What exactly is that?"

"You work with clients, managing their accounts. They're called account executives."

"Do you think I could do that?"

"Maybe—you've worked with different people in several businesses."

"How could I get into the business?"

"Frankly, it's not easy, and you're starting later than most. Right now, it's pretty tight at my agency, but I could make some calls to get you interviews at a few other firms—if you want me to."

"I do, definitely. I'd be grateful to you, Dave."

"Give me a couple of days, and I'll get back to you with some contacts. But, Barry—don't get too excited. I don't know if any of this will work out."

"I won't get my hopes too high."

I called around but came up with only one person who agreed to talk to Barry. Doris Larson was the marketing director of a midsize chain of family restaurants. I had known Doris for about four years. Barry followed through and was able to arrange an interview with Doris. About two weeks later, I received a call from Doris Larson. She said that she was seriously considering Barry to fill the position of advertising coordinator. Doris asked me what I could tell her about Barry.

"I knew him in college, Doris, but I haven't seen much of him since. I can tell you he was a real business junkie back then—way more into financial stuff than any of us. He's kind of banged around, but I have the feeling that he's ready for a permanent gig. What does an advertising coordinator do?"

"We've got thirty-two restaurants in the Midwest. The AC is responsible for making sure that every one of our restaurants properly implements the national advertising campaign as well as listening to any of the individual operator's concerns and communicating those concerns to me. As you might have figured, the job requires a lot of travel and schmoozing with the individual restaurant operators. Dave, do you think Barry could to this job?"

I certainly wasn't sure, but I answered with apparent conviction that I did indeed believe Barry would be an excellent advertising coordinator.

Doris responded, "He's a little pushy—almost arrogant—but that might be what this job requires. You know, the restaurant operators are a tough lot. They'll eat a meek type alive. Barry just may be a good fit. I'm taking a chance, but I'm inclined to offer him the job."

I told Doris I was sure that Barry would do fine. Actually, I wasn't close to sure.

So, Barry got the job as advertising coordinator. I felt that I had done a good deed, and when Doris called me two months later to tell me that Barry was doing well, I was relieved. Maybe this would work out well after all.

Over the next six months, I only saw Barry twice. Once for lunch and another time when I happened to run into him in the men's clothing department at Marshall Fields. We did talk a few times on the phone. My impression was that Barry was in good spirits. So I was shocked when Doris Larson phoned me to say that she had fired Barry.

"I thought that a he was doing great. What happened?" I asked.

"I'm not sure, Dave. Funny because we just gave Barry a really good six-month review and a nice raise. That's when the trouble started."

"What do you mean?"

"Barry was very unhappy with the size of the raise. I mean, he was indignant. Told me it was insulting."

"Did you have any indication that he felt he was underpaid?"

"Not a whisper. And, Dave, just so you know, the raise was the max—20 percent."

"I don't get it."

"I certainly don't. And I'll tell you something else. Barry was like a different person. He was angry and belligerent. He actually screamed at me that the company had taken advantage of him. Said he was sick of the constant traveling. That he was tired of working for cheapskates. That's the word he used."

"Jesus!"

"I didn't have a choice. I had to fire him. Dave, I'm not a psychiatrist, but this guy needs one."

"I don't know what to say. I'm sorry."

"Me too. Dave, if Barry is your friend, you should talk to him. Something not good is going on with him."

———«(O)»———

After several of my calls to Barry went unanswered, he finally got back to me. He sounded very upset and said that he didn't want to talk on the phone. Somewhat reluctantly, he agreed to meet me that night for a drink.

Barry was about a half hour late for our appointment and I was almost ready to leave when the maitre d' showed him to our window booth. He didn't look good—his complexion was pasty, and he obviously hadn't shaved in days. Although it was a warm summer night, he wore a full-length trench coat. I could tell that he was nervous, and he didn't make eye contact when he spoke to me. Before I could even greet him, Barry said, "Let's get something to drink."

"Sure, what do you want?"

"A vodka martini on the rocks—Absolute."

I ordered him a martini and a Heineken for me.

"What the hell happened, Barry?"

"It's simple. I did everything they asked me to do and much more. They told me that I was doing a great job. And, Dave, they promised me a big raise."

"Doris told me they gave you a big bump—20 percent."

"Yeah, 20 percent up from slave wages. I'm not going to take that treatment. Fuck them!"

"Doris told me that she didn't have any warning that you were unhappy."

"She should have paid closer attention."

"Did you tell anybody at the company how you felt?"

"Nobody asked me."

"Barry, if you didn't say anything, how were they supposed to know you were bummed out about the job?"

"They should have taken the initiative. They should have seen that I was way above this job."

"Man, you were there for six months. Obviously they were pleased with your performance, or they wouldn't have given you the big raise. I'm guessing that they had big plans for you."

"When? In ten years? I can do Doris's job right now— better than she can."

"My God, Barry, slow down. You can't expect them—any company—to promote you from an entry-level position to top dog in a matter of months."

"Well, maybe they should have started me higher."

"Barry, you may remember this job was how you got into the ad business. You were damn happy to get the job."

"Okay, so I got it, and I nailed the job."

"Barry, I'm not saying that you didn't. I'm just saying that you way the hell overreacted when they didn't anoint you head of the department after only six months. In the real world, it doesn't work like that."

"Well, maybe it should."

"We seem to be going around in circles."

"Yeah, and I could use another drink."

It went on like this for another hour. After Barry gulped two more vodka martinis and I had nursed another Heineken, it was clear to me that this conversation was going nowhere and that Barry was increasingly inarticulate and unreasonable. Finally, exasperated, I told Barry that my advice was for him to apologize to Doris Larson, and I reminded him that he would need her recommendation for any other job.

"I don't wanner goddamn recondation. I'm own man. To hell wid everbody."

With this, my old pledge brother rose unsteadily from our booth and stumbled from the restaurant into the bustle of the warm summer night on Rush Street. I caught a view

HARVEY POOL

of Barry through the window and could not suppress the thought that he looked like a bum lunging down the street wearing his ridiculous trench coat.

═══◉═══

After that failed meeting, Barry disappeared. For six years nobody I knew either saw or heard from or about him. Then there was a rumor that he had moved to Florida, but there was nothing to confirm that story. Frankly, I didn't think much about Barry Simon. Life, as it always does, moved along. My oldest, Dean, was about to celebrate his bar mitzvah; South Vietnam fell to the Viet Cong; the Cubs again didn't get close to the World Series; everyone was talking about the size of the shark in the movie Jaws; everywhere, you heard Elton John's "Lucy in the Sky with Diamonds;" my wife was reading Ragtime by E. L. Doctorow; an associate and I bought the ad agency where we had worked for several years. I would be forty the next month.

Our ad agency had outgrown its space in the Wrigley Building, and I had an appointment with a real estate broker to check out larger digs in a building on Wacker Drive. I figured that I'd walk six blocks to my appointment, but it had just started to rain, so I hailed a taxi.

The Yellow Cab pulled over, and I got in and gave the driver the address. "Got it," he acknowledged without turning around as he moved into traffic. The first spatter of heavy raindrops resounded on the roof like a jazz drumbeat. We had gone only about a block when the taxi driver turned to me.

── 198 ──

"Hi, Dave, It's Barry. Barry Simon," he said with a giggle that brought back old memories.

"My God! Barry. I can't believe it. It's like seeing a ghost. What are you doing in Chicago?"

"Driving a cab. Hey, Dave, I didn't mean to freak you out. I recognized you when you hailed me."

"I heard you were living in Florida."

"I was—in Miami until six weeks ago."

"What were you doing in Miami?"

"Well, I moved down there four years ago and got back in the real estate business. Things were going really well until a couple of months ago, and then bam."

"What happened?"

"Let's just say I trusted my partners too much. I lost my house, my car, all my money—I got out of town with the shirt on my back, and that's about all."

"Jesus, Barry, I'm sorry to hear that."

"Thanks. Anyway, I figured I'd come back here for a while to kind of recharge my batteries. And the next time I won't get into bed with partners who totally screwed me. The sons of bitches left me holding the bag while they pocketed all the cash."

"Couldn't you sue them, call the cops—something?"

"I tried, but these thieves had planned this real good. Turns out there was nothing I could do."

"Barry, that's awful."

"Don't worry, Dave. I'll get back. I'm not going to let some bad guys—bad luck—keep me down. I'm not planning on driving this taxi for long."

Now we were at my destination. I handed Barry my business

card and told him to call me if I could help. Barry got out of the taxi to open my door and to hold an umbrella over me against the rain. We shook hands. As I ran to the lobby of the Wacker Drive building, two thoughts occurred to me: Barry had asked me nothing about my life, and he had come to look quite like his once esteemed father, Lawrence, only shorter.

I replayed the strange meeting over and over in my mind that mostly sleepless night. Did I believe Barry's sad story? The next morning, I called an old friend in Miami who was a lawyer. I asked him if he could check out Barry T. Simon, who had worked in the real estate business there. My friend told me that the best way to get the information I wanted was to hire a private investigator and that he could recommend a good one, Larry Kilaher. I called Kilaher and explained what I was looking for. Kilaher said that he thought he could help and gave me an estimate of what his services would cost. Three days later, Kilaher called me.

"Mr. Markoff, Larry Kilaher. I believe that I have the information that you requested regarding Barry T. Simon."

"That's great. So, what's the story?"

"I was able to identify the real estate development company that Mr. Simon worked for. He was not a partner, Mr. Markoff. His title was assistant comptroller."

"I see."

"In any event, the information that Mr. Simon gave you is completely contradicted by the real estate development company, Levitt & Adams Builders—a firm that has been operating here in the Miami area for over thirty year. They suggested that I contact their attorney for any other information that I might need. Luckily, that attorney is known to me.

I've done work for their firm. Anyway, I called Jack Kantor at Dewitt, Kelly & Kanter. Jack not only confirmed what Levitt & Adams told me regarding Mr. Simon but said that they were about to contact the district attorney to charge Mr. Simon with grand theft, among other crimes."

"What exactly did they say Barry did?"

"Simply stated, that he stole money—more specifically, embezzled about $34,000, perhaps more."

"Are they after Barry? Is he, what's the word, a fugitive?"

"No, evidently Mr. Simon reimbursed them $10,000 and agreed to repay the remainder over a period of three years. So, Levitt & Adams did not press charges. They just fired him."

I thanked Mr. Kilaher for his services. He told me that he would send me a written report along with his invoice. Then I told my secretary to hold all my calls. I gazed out my twenty-third story window at the flurry of activity on Michigan Avenue and at the great lake gleaming in the morning sun, and I thought about Barry Simon. I did not understand him—what he had become. I tried not to judge him. What a sad life. I pitied him, and I contemplated what fate had led my one-time pledge brother, now in midlife and not quite a felon, to ply the taxi trade on the streets of the city of his promising youth.

———— ((●)) ————

As it turned out, our brief taxi conversation was the last contact I ever had with Barry.

The next three years sped by in a blur.

The news, meager and unsubstantiated, was that Barry may have moved to Los Angeles. If that was true, in my imagination I created a happy-ending story for Barry. He had reunited with his still-beautiful mother. He reinvented himself and prospered perhaps in the movie business. Life was good. I clung to that convenient fairy tale. It seemed the best possible outcome. Then reality, as it often does, kicked me in the head. I learned that Barry had been involved in a check-kiting scheme in Los Angeles and had fled to Mexico or somewhere else. No one was sure.